The Leaders'

Deadly Venoms

Bishop
Orrin K. Pullings

Acknowledgements

As with any major project, it takes a team to build the finished product. I want to extend my personal and sincere thanks to:

Elder Tawana Wright, Chelsea McGhee, Minister Lisa Arnold, Elder Lydia Jones, Prophetess Kelly Crews, my five children: Orrin Jr., Elijah, James, Zacchaeus, and Medina, thank you all for your support.

Dedications

I dedicate this book to the Queen of my heart, the most beautiful woman on the inside and the outside and in the whole world, my amazing wife, **Medina**. I think back on our journey, and I am amazed at how far we have come. Thank you for working and growing with me and never giving up on me! You continue to push and remind me every day of what God has given me. You are the hardest working woman in the Kingdom of God. I am the most fortunate and blessed man on the planet with you by my side. Medina, thank you, I will love you forever.

I would also like to dedicate this book to my father, **Pastor James Pullings, Jr.** You were the first person to license me to preach, and my first role model. Not only are you my father, you are my spiritual covering, my mentor, and my friend. In watching your example, I have learned what a good leader is and how a good lead should operate. Thank you for seeing who I was, before I knew who I was, and leading me down the correct path. I am the leader that I am today, because of everything that you imparted into me. I love you, Dad.

To my mother, **Esther Pullings, y**ou are the first woman that I ever loved and you have continuously prayed, pushed and believed in me. I know I was the child that gave you the most problems, but your fervent prayers have molded me into the man that I am today. I take pride in knowing that you can count on me, and I can count on you, for anything. Your love and support means the world to me, and I will cherish you forever. I love you mommy!

Bishop Derrick Hutchins, thank you for teaching me ministerial conduct, dress code, character, and being my inspiration to fill my call and assignment in my pastoral ministry. I am forever grateful for the years that you mentored me, allowed me to stay in Columbia, SC with you, drive for you, and travel with you just holding your briefcase and travel bag from church to church. You have taught me a lot. Thank you for giving me space in your life and ministry. I love you.

Bishop Frank O. White, I want to thank you for seeing the God and call in my life at an early age. Thank you for ordaining me at 19 years old. It is because of you and your ministry that I am able to stand over 25 years later, fulfill, and complete the assignment that God has given me. I love you and thank you for your faithfulness, encouragement and support.

Archbishop Roy E. Brown, how can I thank you enough for seeing the overseer and the bishop that God ordained me to be. As a young man, you taught me so many things about people, life, and ministry. You were there for me during some of my toughest battles as a new pastor. I will be forever grateful for the spiritual father and mentor that you are and have been to me. I hope that I will never let you down. Thank you for consecrating me as a bishop in the Lord's church.

Endorsements

Reading *"The Leaders' 7 Deadly Venoms"*, I couldn't help but to remember the many battles, trials, attacks, and ultimately the victories that Bishop Orrin and I have seen over the past 20 years in ministry! Wow! I'm so thankful to God who has given us the VICTORY! We NEEDED a book like this coming up! Lol! It surely would've been a great help. Bishop Orrin gives leaders and congregations a deeper look into the warfare of a leader, pitfalls to watch out for, exposes the tactics of the enemy, and gives strategies for winning! There are so many pastors/leaders silently suffering and hurting. I am certain this book will help many people. Every pastor/leader needs a copy of this book! Every member should be armed with a copy. I'm so proud of my husband's courage to pen this script! I've watched him navigate through so many battles. Preaching his best sermons during the worst of times! Building despite of all. Marching forward because of the duty of the call! Don't waste time in getting your copy! This book will transcend your life!

Medina Pullings

A familiar refrain from pastors and church leaders is, "Why is this person (or group) so adamantly opposed to what I'm attempting to accomplish? I'm just trying to help people!" Relentless opposition is at best a distraction, and at worst can cause a God-given vision to be compromised or even canceled.

Bishop Orrin K. Pullings new book, *The Leaders' 7 Deadly Venoms: Conquering 21st Century Opposition* gives you invaluable insight into the reasons for the opposition you experience, as well as strategies to overcome it. Opposition is inevitable, but it doesn't have to be fatal to your vision or your personal well-being. Bishop Pullings provides the antidote to the venoms every successful leader will encounter.

Dr. Rod Parsley
Pastor, World Harvest Church
Columbus, Ohio

Table of Contents

Acknowledgements

Dedications

Endorsements

About the Author

Chapter One

The Spirit of Venom

The word venom, in its simplest explanation, means poison. Often times, the two words are used interchangeably. Venom has two definitions; one of which expresses the natural science of what venom really is and another to express a more psychological state of being that is used.

Definition:

VENOM: 1) A poisonous substance secreted by animals such as snakes, spiders, and scorpions and typically injected into prey or aggressors by biting or stinging.

2) Extreme malice and bitterness shown in someone's attitude, speech, or actions.

The spirit of venom is a psychological state of using past hurt and pain as a catalyst of venom.

It is also a defense mechanism that people use every time they notice something familiar coming along. People will often "throw up a wall of venom," as a means of protecting themselves. Venom is also the backlash that someone might receive, as a result of someone else's actions. You see, venom is a major form of defense, almost like putting a wall up. Most people that have any type of venom, also have been used or mistrusted by someone else in the past. You see this often in the case of someone that may get into a relationship with someone new, but holds onto the offenses of the last person.

When the Word of God speaks of poison or venom, it uses both definitions in correlation with each other. The insects mentioned in scripture are used, as metaphors, to depict the behavior of humans and the wicked one, not the righteous.

Such is the case with Psalm 58:1-4:

Psalm 58:1-4 NASB

"Do you indeed speak righteousness, O gods?
Do you judge uprightly, O sons of men? 2 No, in
heart you work unrighteousness; on earth
you weigh out the violence of your hands. 3 The
wicked are estranged from the womb;
these who speak lies go astray from birth.
4 They have venom like the venom of a serpent;
like a deaf cobra that stops up its ear,"

Psalm 140:3 Parallel

"³They make their tongues as sharp as a snake's bite; viper's venom is under their lips. Selah"

Romans 3:13 Parallel

"¹³Their throat is an open grave; they deceive with their tongues. Vipers' venom is under their lips."

Venom or poison is lodged inside of insects such as spiders, bees, snakes, and scorpions. Their venom is used as a defense mechanism for the prey and predators. In the expression of psychological thoughts, venom is used by humans against the character of another person and even used to demean, undermine and dethrone or remove from a place of authority and influence in the minds of people. Some are blissfully unaware of the negative impact that they have on those around them and others seem to derive satisfaction from creating chaos and pushing people's buttons. Either way, they create unnecessary complexity, strife and worst of all, stress.

It is hard to think that venom is used as a defense mechanism, when it is used from a psychological perspective, but it is. Many people go through life, without taking the responsibility for their personal self-care and mental health. Mental health is so important and needed for everyone. I do not know one person that has never been through some traumatic event (i.e. physical abuse, sexual abuse, verbal abuse, death/loss of a loved one, financial hardship, loss of a house or car, loss of employment, divorce, etc.). When these events happen in life and a person does not take responsibility or self-care for them self, a level of hurt, pain, situational depression, and twisted perspectives can evolve; which is usually expressed through the vehicle of venom.

The lack of self-care, for such traumatic events, can bring on medical conditions such as depression, anxiety, panic attacks and post-traumatic stress disorder. We use defense mechanisms to cope with unpleasant emotions. They give us a way to circumvent our reality.

Thinking about venom brings me to the statement that, "hurt people, hurt people." Most people that spew venom or lash out at others have somehow been emotionally or mentally crippled, at some point. If you listen carefully or study their pattern of behavior, it can be readily recognized. Sometimes, those who hurt us are usually hurting themselves and their pain may be so strong that they are not even aware that they are hurting us.

These types of people are so chronically unhappy and are stuck feeling victimized and lacking awareness of the impact of their own actions and words. They don't realize that they are co-creating their problems. They're often angry, frustrated and highly critical of others and feel that their problems deserve immediate attention, without regard for the world around them. In other words, they believe that their urgency is your emergency.

This is where the spirit of venom begins to operate.

These are some critical signs in people that would operate with a spirit of venom:

Bitter people often transfer their anger over to their family and closest friends. Those around them become the recipients of maliciousness and fits of rage, because they have unknowingly become the recipients of the person's hatred. They will regularly put you in a position where you have to choose between them and something else and you will always feel obliged to choose them. They will wait until you have a commitment, then they will unfold the drama.

Hurt people interpret words that are spoken to them through the lens of their pain. Because of their pain, simple words are often misunderstood to mean something negative towards them. They misinterpret actions and words to mean the worst-case scenario and view things from a negative outlook. It almost resembles a victim mentality, but sometimes they just cannot see past their own past pain or life traumas. This can cripple any new relationship. They are very defensive and not willing to open up to listen to the truth behind the words being spoken.

Venomous people interpret every action as a wrong motive or evil intent behind other

people's actions towards them. They are extremely sensitive and act out of pain instead of reality. They go into "attack mode." It can almost seem as if they are paranoid. They don't trust anyone and everyone is always out to get them. They feel as if others are always talking about them behind their backs. It causes intense feelings of distrust and leads to covert hostility.

People that carry venom in their spirit, heart, and mind, often portray themselves as victims and carry a "victim spirit." Venomous people can cry "racism," "sexism," "homophobia," or often use the words "unjust" or "unfair" to describe the way they are being treated, even if there is no truth to this. (That is not to say that sometimes there really is racism or sexism in some instances; this is used as an example.) Victims are tough to identify because you initially empathize with their problems.

However, as time passes, you begin to realize that their "time of need" is all the time. Victims actively push away any personal responsibility by making every speed bump they encounter into an uncrossable mountain. They don't see tough times as opportunities to learn and grow, instead, they see them as an out. There's an old saying, "Pain is inevitable, but suffering is optional." It perfectly captures the toxicity of the victim, who chooses to suffer every time.

They often alienate others, totally rely on one chosen person, and wonder why no one is there for them. It is a tactic to get attention. Venomous people love to get attention. They often continually hurt the ones they love and need the most with their self-destructive behavior. If you feel as though you're the only one contributing to the relationship, you're probably right. Venomous people have a way of sending out the vibe that you owe them something.

They also have a way of taking from you or doing something that hurts you, then maintaining they were doing it all for you. This is particularly common in workplaces or relationships, where the balance of power is off.

Venomous people have the emotional maturity of the age they received their undealt with hurt. For example, if a girl was raped by a man when she was 12 years old, unless she forgives that man and allows Christ to heal her heart in that particular area of her life, her emotional growth will stop. A lack of maturity is one of the easiest signs to spot in people who have experienced significant trauma. The bad things that happen do not always leave someone frozen in their maturity tracks. Bad things stunt maturity when they cause a person to live in fear, which we often call stress, anxiety, or post-traumatic stress.

Even when she reaches her later years, she may still have the emotional maturity of a 12-year-old. The hurtful act or betrayal will sometimes trigger them to return to the event unless, they are delivered and able to let it go.

People that carry venom are often frustrated, depressed, and act irrational because past pain continually spills over into their present consciousness. In many instances, they may not even be aware of why they are continually frustrated or depressed, because they have coped with pain by compartmentalizing it or layering it with other things over time. They will be completely fine one day, and the next, you will be wondering what you have done to upset them. There often isn't anything obvious that will explain the change of attitude, you just know something is not right. They might be sad, cold, or cranky, and when you ask if there is something wrong, the answer will likely be "nothing," but they will give you just enough to let you know that there is something irritating them.

The "just enough" might be a heaving sigh, a raised eyebrow, or a cold shoulder. When this happens, you might find yourself making excuses for them or doing everything you can to make them happy. The layers of pain causes years of bitterness to build. No matter how successful or elevated they become, they will always be overwhelmed because they have not dealt with themselves and the underlying issue.

Venom causes people to often erupt with inappropriate emotion, because particular words, actions, or past circumstances "touch" and "trigger" past wounds. I have been in situations with people in which there was a gross overreaction to a word I spoke or an action that was taken. Although I was shocked and thought this reaction came "out of left field," it was really the person responding to an accumulation of years of hurt and pain that could not help but to spill over in various areas of their lives. They use these common phrases "you always ..." or "you never ..." and it is hard to defend yourself against this form of manipulation.

Toxic people have a way of drawing on the one time "you did not," or the one time "you did," as evidence of your shortcomings. When you are trying to resolve something important to you, venomous people will bring in irrelevant details from five arguments ago. The problem with this is that before you know it, you are arguing about something you did six months ago, and you are still defending yourself, rather than dealing with the issue at hand. Somehow, it just always seems to end up about what you have done to them. Do not buy into the argument. You will not win and you do not need to.

The spirit of venom punishes honesty and rewards lying. It obligates your agreement no matter what. These types of people are unhappy when you disagree with them. They need you to agree with them. You can tell by the pressure you feel to do things their way.

This can take various forms from anger, to cold shoulders, to being excluded from inner circles. Arguments ensue that never end.

If you finally see the light and agree with them, they are happy, especially if you do so sooner rather than later. Sometimes, this is called "stroking their ego."

Their delight at your agreement is how you are rewarded for lying. Followers who cooperate with these people are either avoiding conflict or manipulating them, more often the former. The conflict that arises from being honest is not worth it. Working under this habit can make staff feel low self-esteem, as their confidence is undermined. These weak people start living in a bubble insulated from opposing points of view.

Venomous behavior is found in the narcissist. Narcissistic Personality Disorder involves arrogant behavior, a lack of empathy for other people, and a need for admiration, all of which must be consistently evident at work, and in relationships. These narcissistic people are frequently described as cocky, self-centered, manipulative, and demanding. They are boastful or pretentious. Narcissists often monopolize conversations, belittle, or look down on people they perceive as inferior, and feel a sense of entitlement, and when they don't receive special treatment, they may become impatient or angry. They are very damaging to anyone they come into relationship with.

They are venomous in a very selfish way. The narcissist has trouble handling anything that may be perceived as criticism. They may have secret feelings of insecurity, shame, vulnerability, and humiliation. To feel better they may react with rage or contempt, and try to belittle the other person to make themselves appear superior.

Here are three definitive words that are common when dealing with the spirit of venom.

DISPLACEMENT - In displacement, you transfer your original feelings that would get you in trouble (usually anger) away from the person who is the target of your rage to a more helpless and harmless victim. The victim has no idea why you are angry, but they are the recipient of your hurtful and abusive behavior.

PROJECTION - This is more common than we recognize. When someone is not satisfied with himself or herself or insecure with an area of their life, they will call awareness to the issue by accusing someone else or placing undesirable feelings or emotions onto someone else, rather than admitting to or dealing with the unwanted feelings.

REACTION FORMATION - This is expressing the opposite of your inner feelings in your outward behavior, causing extreme pain and damage to the person involved. Here is an example; you secretly harbor lustful feelings toward someone you should probably stay away from. You do not want to admit to these feelings, so you instead express the very opposite of those feelings. This object of your lust now becomes the object of your bitter hatred.

Venomous people most often:

1. Have you guessing what version of them you will be speaking to or dealing with.

2. Manipulate everything to their favor.

3. Do not own their feelings.

4. Never apologize.

5. Make you over prove yourself.

6. Are always there in a crisis, but never want to celebrate.

7. Leave conversations unfinished.

8. Use very harsh and angry tones.

9. Bring up irrelevant details.

10. Focus on how you "speak" and ignore your conversation content.

11. Exaggerate.

12. Are very judgmental.

While of course, some venom is used to defend and protect, it is more than common to see venom used in these malicious ways. It does not matter what capacity you serve in or the title you have, venom is commonplace, and very prevalent in the church.

Bullying and intimidation are other great descriptive words when it comes to defining venom. You may have been teased, gossiped about, shouted at, hit, defamed, backed into a corner, intimidated, and unjustly punished, and your reaction might be, "WHY?"

Here are some crucial signs that a venomous person affects you:

1. You are emotionally affected by their drama.

2. You dread (or fear) being around them.

3. You are exhausted or you feel angry while you are with them or after your interaction.

4. You feel bad or ashamed about yourself.

5. You are stuck in a cycle of trying to rescue, fix, or care for them.

6. The other person does not respect the word "no" as a complete sentence.

7. When you are with them, you feel like you are "walking on eggshells."

8. You ignore your own values.

9. You emotionally "check-out."

10. You feel like you are being controlled.

Why are people so cruel with you and venomous towards each other? Why do some people seem to actually enjoy venomous behavior?

If you are like most people, your immediate answer might be something along the lines of, "because they're bad people," "because they're psychopaths/sociopaths," "because they're evil," "because some people are just like that!"

While these answers are normal and widespread, they are nevertheless, two-dimensional, and narrow in outlook. While such answers would have sufficed for our younger childlike selves, it is time that we develop a more seasoned understanding of why "bad people are bad." We have all had venomous people dust us with their poison. Sometimes, it is more like a drenching. Difficult people are drawn to the reasonable ones and all of us have likely had (or have) at least one person in our lives, who had us bending around ourselves like barbed wire in endless attempts to please them, only to never really get there. Their damage lies in their subtlety and the way they can encompass that classic response, "it's not them, it's me." They can have you questioning your "over-reaction," your "oversensitivity," or your "tendency to misinterpret."

If you are the one who is continually hurt, or the one who is constantly adjusting your own behavior to avoid being hurt, then chances are, it is not you, and it is very much them. Being able to spot their harmful behavior is the first step to minimize their impact. You might not be able to change what they do, but, you can change what you do with it. You have full authority over the spirit of venom. As we continue further in this book, I will teach you how to win against venomous people.

Chapter Two

The Man Moses and His Call to Leadership

Numbers 12:3 NKJV

"3Now the man Moses was very humble, more than all men who were on the face of the earth."

Acts 7:22 NKJV

"22 And Moses was learned in all the wisdom of the Egyptians, and was mighty in words and deeds."

In the book of Numbers, the Bible declared Moses to be a very humble man, but where did his humility and meekness begin? Moses certainly did not start out that way.

Moses had the tenacity and poise to do what God called him to do, because he was never enslaved, nor did he ever see himself a slave. He was a free Hebrew. His people were slaves, but he was not. He was an Egyptian Prince even though he was not born an Egyptian. He was being called by our sovereign Lord but unfortunately, he had feelings of inadequacy.

In studying his story, the relevant question becomes, "where did this humility and meekness that Moses possessed, come from?" It came from God. God imparted this humility into Moses through a series of dramatic life experiences. Moses humility and meekness was worked into him, through the craftiness of the power of God at work in his life. When Moses became a grown man, he suddenly became aware of who he really was and knew that he was a Hebrew.

One day, Moses saw one of his brethren being beaten by an Egyptian, and as a result, he murdered the Egyptian. Fearing that Pharaoh knew about it, Moses fled.

While on the run, Moses met a man by the name of Jethro, a Midian Priest, and later, he married his daughter Zipporah. After 40 years of working for Jethro, Moses had an encounter with God. It was in this encounter that he was told by God himself that he would be the leader of His people, and that he would be used to lead the people out of Egypt. When Moses got back to Egypt, he soon came to the realization that these people, of whom he would be their leader and were his kinsmen, had been enslaved for over 430 years (Exodus 12:40).

This means they were beaten, tortured, and treated with cruelty, and as a result, they were bitter, hurt, and disgruntled. In spite of all of this, God still wanted to deliver them. As a leader, Moses was not greeted with a fruit basket and flowers by a people who were excited to meet his acquaintance. So typically, they were very critical of him and judged everything that he did. They reluctantly followed Moses in fear that they would be captured once again by the Egyptians. However, Moses was the set man that God would use to lead His people.

By this time, Moses had what it took, having being raised and taught by the Royalty of Egypt, Moses had the knowledge and training to lead the people of God. He knew how to deal and respond to Pharaoh and how to get around Egypt. However, there was one more thing that God was getting ready to give Moses, and that was humility. Anyone that is called to lead God's people must develop a level of humility and compassion. Without humility and compassion, it will be very difficult to lead.

When Moses took God at His word, he found that when things got hard, the people turned on him. The people began to murmur and complain at every effort made to bring them to a better place.

Exodus 14:10-12 KJV

"10 And when Pharaoh drew nigh, the children of Israel lifted up their eyes, and, behold, the Egyptians marched after them; and they were sore afraid: and the children of Israel cried out unto the Lord.

11 And they said unto Moses, because there were no graves in Egypt, hast thou taken us away to die in the wilderness? Wherefore hast thou dealt thus with us, to carry us forth out of Egypt?

12 Is not this the word that we did tell thee in Egypt, saying, let us alone, that we may serve the Egyptians? For it had been better for us to serve the Egyptians, than that we should die in the wilderness."

Moses is identified, in Christian literature, as a prototype of Jesus. The name Moses comes from the Hebrew word, "Mashah," which means to draw out. Not only was Moses rescued out of the river by Pharaoh's daughter, but he would be the one to lead the children of Israel out of Egypt. Could it be that the children of Israel continuously released venom against Moses their leader, because of the previous hardship that they had endured? A harsh, coarse, caterwauling Pharaoh ruled them.

They did not fully trust his leadership and were afraid of the outcome.

Isn't it so, in many of our lives today, that when we experience hardship, it takes the love of God to get us to receive something or someone who means us good. Too often when the Lord is trying to bless His people, our perception of what God is doing is tainted and distorted. Moses was the man that God was using. Moses had previously dealt with Pharaoh, in Egypt. He had also told the Egyptians what they could and could not do. They saw the miracle of deliverance from each plague that the Lord placed on the Egyptians. They also saw every miracle that the Lord allowed Moses to perform with the rod, yet, when they got to the Red Sea they were still discontented.

It is very important for individuals not to hold past leadership hurts and disappointments against their new leaders that are God-sent and God ordained. It will only limit their productivity and personal growth. When leadership is God ordained, the leader must have a certain level of trust by those that follow them. In order to achieve that, the individual must be healed from past hardships.

Chapter Three

Jeremiah's Call to Leadership

Jeremiah 1:1-10 KJV

"*¹The words of Jeremiah the son of Hilkiah, of the priests that were in Anathoth in the land of Benjamin:*

² To whom the word of the Lord came in the days of Josiah the son of Amon king of Judah, in the thirteenth year of his reign.

³ It came also in the days of Jehoiakim the son of Josiah king of Judah, unto the end of the eleventh year of Zedekiah the son of Josiah king of Judah, unto the carrying away of Jerusalem captive in the fifth month.

⁴ Then the word of the Lord came unto me, saying,

⁵ Before I formed thee in the belly I knew thee; and before thou camest forth out of the womb I sanctified thee, and I ordained thee a prophet unto the nations.

⁶ Then said I, Ah, Lord God! Behold, I cannot speak: for I am a child.

⁷ But the Lord said unto me, Say not, I am a child: for thou shalt go to all that I shall send thee, and whatsoever I command thee thou shalt speak.

⁸ Be not afraid of their faces: for I am with thee to deliver thee, saith the Lord.

⁹ Then the Lord put forth his hand, and touched my mouth. And the Lord said unto me, Behold, I have put my words in thy mouth.

¹⁰ See, I have this day set thee over the nations and over the kingdoms, to root out, and to pull down, and to destroy, and to throw down, to build, and to plant."

God called Jeremiah, at an early age, to be a leader. However, he was only a young boy and began to look at his age. God told him not to look at his age because He had called him to be a leader. As a young person, sometimes, it is hard to gain respect from people because of your age.

I endured some of my biggest battles, when I was young. I had to prove that I was anointed enough, big enough, bad enough, and bold enough to do the job. There were times when people told me, "I will never follow a young man because young men haven't been through enough in life and haven't experienced enough." However, I was mature enough to know that the Bible says that age should not be considered. I learned in that season, that you cannot minister from your age or experience. And when you are that young, it has to be based solely off scripture. Instead of using life's experiences, it was important for me to rely on the Holy Spirit, the anointing from God and what was showed to me in prayer.

With age comes experience and you can begin to tell more personal stories versus the stories of Meshach, Shadrach and Abednego. As a young leader, you have to have a lot of God to help you maneuver the mental ills of some people that come into your life. God told Jeremiah not to focus on his own abilities, but to focus on God's capabilities. God instructed him that he should go where he was sent and say what he was told to say.

Jeremiah 1:18-19 KJV

"18 For, behold, I have made thee this day a defensed city, and an iron pillar, and brazen walls against the whole land, against the kings of Judah, against the princes thereof, against

the priests thereof, and against the people of the land.

19 And they shall fight against thee; but they shall not prevail against thee; for I am with thee, saith the Lord, to deliver thee."

God puts a fence around those He calls. A defensed city cannot be taken over. It may be attacked, but it cannot be overtaken. Jeremiah was an iron pillar, inflexible, and unyielding. The reason God makes us this way is because there are many spirits that want us to sway and not preach the whole gospel. Instead, they want us to go mainstream, bend a little, and water down the Word of God.

However, God's word was not meant to be that way. A leader in ministry must be 100% secure in their beliefs, have faith in God and His word, and speak the truth. Truth brings trouble. Sometimes, the truth is unattractive to the person that is hearing it. Leadership has to be a bearer of truth, at all times. Even in corporate America, the truth sometimes brings backlash. The truth makes you better, so tell it like it is.

God told Jeremiah, "I will make you a bronze wall." This signifies two metals, copper and tin. Copper is corrosion resistant and sometimes used for water pipes in houses. It is able to withstand years of water without rusting. When you stay close to God, He will keep you from being corroded by your environment. Sometimes, your surroundings can corrode you, but in God that will not happen.

You will learn your limitations and strengths and when God or YOU, the leader, should handle something. Sometimes, there is a blurry line between what a leader does and what God does, but God will make it clear. No matter what Jeremiah dealt with, God would not allow the corruption to corrupt him. God told Jeremiah He would set him over all the high officials over the land, to root out, tear down, destroy, and build again.

Every leader, at some point must tear down things that have been built incorrectly. They have to destroy things that are not in alignment with the vision. Every leader must uproot, tear down, destroy, and build again. There is always a demolition process, before rebuilding.

It is the leader's responsibility to do this. Sometimes, you want to be passive, but what you let go on for too long will get out of control. In other words, what you allow, you promote. Weak leaders allow injustices to continue, while strong leaders will confront the issue. Sometimes as a leader, you have to be confrontational. God gave Jeremiah the power to stand against whoever stood against him.

You cannot be a good leader and be too passive. If a leader does not confront an issue in someone's life that is under him, eventually that leader will be next in line confronting that same problem, from the same person. In other words, the issue will grow all around the leader, until it attempts to confront the leader. As a leader, you should try to confront things that happen, when you see them. If you don't correct people, they only get worse. This is how repeat offenders are birthed. They have no intent to change. The longer someone gets away with doing wrong, the easier it becomes to do wrong and the wrong will elevate to higher levels.

It is important to protect the smallest person that you lead and make sure that everyone is treated correctly. You cannot let bullies rule and reign on your territory, because eventually they will be big enough to bully you. Keep in mind, when someone is corrected during the root out process (correction and rebuke), be sure to also highlight their strengths, as well. You have to build them back up and show them a better way of proceeding and engaging, for the future. Each time I received correction from my parents, after it was over, they would build me back up and show me how to better deal with the situation for the future. Good leaders challenge others to be greater.

Chapter Four

Miriam and Aaron's Venom

Exodus 33:11

"11 So the Lord spoke to Moses face to face, as a man speaks to his friend. And he would return to the camp, but his servant Joshua the son of Nun, a young man, did not depart from the tabernacle."

Miriam and Aaron wanted to be used, in the same capacity as Moses. God did use them, but not to the same magnitude as how He used Moses. God spoke to Moses, face-to-face. God spoke to Moses regarding leadership, direction, areas of focus, destinations, rules of engagement, correction, and more. God often speaks to the leader first, because they have the responsibility of getting the orders of God carried out. For example, the quarterback is a field worker and has to take direction from the coach, in order for the team to win the game.

When I was younger in my first year of pastoring, I had members that were older than me, say, "You have the vision, but God has shown me the way." You should know that when God gives a leader a vision, He also gives them the direction. This person turned out to be one of my greatest oppositions during that time in my life. People will try to manipulate you, but the leader must take direction from God and not people when it comes to the overall game plan.

Miriam and Aaron began to speak out against Moses, because his wife was a Cushite. They asked if the Lord had only spoken through Moses and not through them, as well.

Numbers 12:1-15 KJV

"And Miriam and Aaron spake against Moses because of the Ethiopian woman whom he had married: for he had married an Ethiopian woman.

[2] And they said, Hath the Lord indeed spoken only by Moses? hath he not spoken also by us? And the Lord heard it.

[3] (Now the man Moses was very meek, above all the men which were upon the face of the earth.)

[4] And the Lord spake suddenly unto Moses, and unto Aaron, and unto Miriam, Come out ye

three unto the tabernacle of the congregation. And they three came out.

⁵ And the Lord came down in the pillar of the cloud, and stood in the door of the tabernacle, and called Aaron and Miriam: and they both came forth.

⁶ And he said, hear now my words: If there be a prophet among you, I the Lord will make myself known unto him in a vision, and will speak unto him in a dream.

⁷ My servant Moses is not so, who is faithful in all mine house.

⁸ With him will I speak mouth to mouth, even apparently, and not in dark speeches; and the similitude of the Lord shall he behold: wherefore then were ye not afraid to speak against my servant Moses?

⁹ And the anger of the Lord was kindled against them; and he departed.

¹⁰ And the cloud departed from off the tabernacle; and, behold, Miriam became leprous, white as snow: and Aaron looked upon Miriam, and, behold, she was leprous.

¹¹ *And Aaron said unto Moses, Alas, my lord, I beseech thee, lay not the sin upon us, wherein we have done foolishly, and wherein we have sinned.*

¹² *Let her not be as one dead, of whom the flesh is half consumed when he cometh out of his mother's womb.*

¹³ *And Moses cried unto the Lord, saying, Heal her now, O God, I beseech thee.*

¹⁴ *And the Lord said unto Moses, if her father had but spit in her face, should she not be ashamed seven days? Let her be shut out from the camp seven days, and after that let her be received in again.*

¹⁵ *And Miriam was shut out from the camp seven days: and the people journeyed not till Miriam was brought in again."*

The Lord heard when they questioned His choice of leader. Moses was very humble and the Lord told Moses to invite Miriam and Aaron out with him. The Lord began to speak to all of them regarding how He spoke to his leader, Moses, versus how He spoke to Miriam and

Aaron. God used Miriam and Aaron, but not on the same level that He used Moses. When they found Moses at a low point for marrying a Cushite woman, they used that as an opportunity to undermine their leader, based on the personal decision that he made.

Every leader has a personal life, outside of ministry, that is between them and God. No other person has a say in that. Every leader must have the ability to come out of their job description and live their life and not be judged based on their personal choices that are outside of sin. No leader's life is going to be 100% pleasing to a group of people. There are too many personalities to satisfy them all. Because we are not a God to people, certain things should be off limits. Leaders must learn to balance public opinion, versus their own likes. Public opinion will have you driving a Cadillac every year, even though you do not personally like them.

Miriam and Aaron judged Moses personal taste. Never undermine your leader, based on the way God uses you, versus them. The clear distinction was that Moses was the one to lead the children of Israel to the promise. His line of communication with God, was very special and unlike any other. There are some that try to bring light to areas in a leader's life, that they feel are imperfect. However, I have not found a leader yet, that is perfect. But, God can do a perfect work through them, in spite of themselves.

There is a penalty to be paid when you go against ordained leadership. Miriam's penalty for speaking against Moses was leprosy. The very leader Miriam went against prayed for the leprosy to be stripped from her body and God honored his prayer (Numbers 12:13). Pray for your leadership and God will correct them. God fixes his leaders, not people. God hired them, not people.

Aaron and Miriam discredited Moses because of his personal choice. But, had he made the choice they liked, there would not have been a problem. That is why we are all blessed differently, we are unique. Marry whomever you want, forget about the people's choice. YOU have to go to bed and wake up with that person and the people are not around when that happens. A leader's life must be separate. Anyone that goes against that has the spirit of Miriam and Aaron.

On the other hand, there are certain things that leaders should not do either. Leaders should not be putting people together. One pastor I know only allows people within their congregation to marry each other. This is wrong. A person's mate may not be within your congregation. People cannot control people and people cannot control leaders. Leaders should lead people into a greater place with God and the higher knowledge of His son Jesus Christ.

As a leader, I have found it to be too much work to figure out who is dating and who is getting married. That is too involved. Lead them to the Holy Spirit and He will lead them. Teach them the truth and the truth will govern their decision making for everyday life, marriage, family, business, etc.

Chapter Five

Potiphar's Wife's Venom

This no name Egyptian's wife, of an officer of Pharaoh's, only purpose in the Bible was to prove the strength and endurance of a man who was completely supported by God, Joseph. This was a man who would represent the nation of God, the way that God intended him to: resisting temptation.

Genesis 39:6-21 NKJV

"⁶ Thus he left all that he had in Joseph's hand, and he did not know what he had except for the bread which he ate.

Now, Joseph was handsome in form and appearance.

⁷ And it came to pass after these things that his master's wife cast longing eyes on Joseph, and she said, "Lie with me." ⁸ But he refused and said to his master's wife, "Look, my master does not know what is with me in the house, and he has committed all that he has to my hand. ⁹ There is no one greater in this house than I, nor has he kept back anything from me but you, because you are his wife. How then can I do this great wickedness, and sin against God?"

[10] *So it was, as she spoke to Joseph day by day, that he did not heed her, to lie with her or to be with her.* [11] *But it happened about this time, when Joseph went into the house to do his work, and none of the men of the house was inside,* [12] *that she caught him by his garment, saying, "Lie with me." But he left his garment in her hand, and fled and ran outside.* [13] *And so it was, when she saw that he had left his garment in her hand and fled outside,* [14] *that she called to the men of her house and spoke to them, saying, "See, he has brought in to us a Hebrew to mock us. He came in to me to lie with me, and I cried out with a loud voice.* [15] *And it happened, when he heard that I lifted my voice and cried out, that he left his garment with me, and fled and went outside."*

[16] *So she kept his garment with her until his master came home.* [17] *Then she spoke to him with words like these, saying, "The Hebrew servant whom you brought to us came in to me to mock me;* [18] *so it happened, as I lifted my voice and cried out, that he left his garment with me and fled outside."*

19 So it was, when his master heard the words which his wife spoke to him, saying, "Your servant did to me after this manner," that his anger was aroused. 20 Then Joseph's master took him and put him into the prison, a place where the king's prisoners were confined. And he was there in the prison. 21 But the Lord was with Joseph and showed him mercy, and He gave him favor in the sight of the keeper of the prison."

The spirit of Potiphar's wife is described as the attraction to authority. These spirits only want leaders because of their position or what has been given to them. Authority turned Potiphar's wife on. Potiphar left everything he had in Joseph's care. In stature, Joseph was well built and handsome.

However, you do not have to be handsome in order to have someone attracted to your power. Potiphar's wife was attracted to Joseph and his power, after all of the authority was given to him by Potiphar. Joseph did very well in his position.

You must know that people will take notice
of you when you do a good or excellent job.
This applies to anyone in a position of power.
Doing well attracts the spirit of Potiphar's wife,
a woman that loved strong leadership. The
more that was given to Joseph, the more it
turned her on.

His authority made her physically attracted
to him and she gave Joseph an open invitation
to go to bed with her and he refused. The bible
says in the book of Genesis that Potiphar's wife
had attempted to seduce him at other times
and he resisted.

Not only was Joseph tempted by Potiphar's
wife, but Joseph may have also been tempted
by outside sources. The temptation of the devil
and foreign cultures that served other Gods
and cultures of different practices may have
also tried to persuade him. Joseph was in Egypt
under Egyptian rule and government.
Potiphar's wife served Baal.

I can imagine that Joseph was resisting many
practices that were not of his culture and
persuasion. Joseph was a man in authority,
under authority. He said no to Potiphar's wife

for two reasons, one, to not sin against God, and two, not to offend Potiphar. He was a man of standard and principle.

Although there is no excuse for Potiphar's wife in her attempts to seduce Joseph, she is discussed in Christian literature to possibly have been neglected by her husband, Potiphar. Joseph is the next best thing, because her husband has placed all things in the household, under Joseph's rule. Surely being with Joseph would not only satisfy her physically, but also make a statement to her husband. However, this is only a theory, the scriptures do not support this thought.

Potiphar's wife's venom is the venom of rejection. "How could he not want me, I am Potiphar's wife." However, Joseph's standard was greater than what Potiphar's wife could offer him. Because Joseph told her no, she ripped his clothes as he escaped her, and used his clothing as evidence against him. She then told the servants that he attempted to assault her. When Potiphar came home, she told him the same story, blaming Joseph for a crime that he did not commit. Potiphar became angry and threw Joseph into prison. However, God was with Joseph while he was in prison and gave him favor with the prison guards. When God's hands are on you, there is nothing that can stop it. Joseph was supposed to be promoted, so even when he went to prison, he was given the task to run the prison. No matter where you are, and regardless of the circumstances presented before you, God can elevate you.

When you have an appointment with destiny, plans will be ruined just to get you out of your comfort zone. Keep in mind, demonic interruptions will bring about divine connections. Some people are so full of themselves, that telling them no is the worst thing that you can do. This all worked out for Joseph's good.

All leaders must be aware that some people will want you because of the power and anointing that you possess. There must be integrity present when you have these gifts or otherwise, this is an accident waiting to happen. Every leader must have sexual discipline. If not, there is always someone there ready, willing, and able, just because you are in charge.

For instance, Bubba with no teeth, bad breath, crossed eyes, a potbelly, watermelon head, and two left feet is not ordinarily attractive, however, if you give him a position and some authority, the women will flock to him. This is called authority attraction.

No matter what the position is, you are a direct target for the advances of someone that has the spirit of Potiphar's wife. Remain balanced and know that you are nothing without the Lord. They are not necessarily attracted to you, but attracted to the power that you possess.

There are certain spirits assigned to overtake leaders. You must be aware of this. Demonic spirits are assigned to your anointing.

Chapter Six

The Spirit of Jezebel and Delilah Venom: The Power of Manipulation

2 Kings 9:30 NIV

"³⁰ Then Jehu went to Jezreel. When Jezebel heard about it, she put on eye makeup, arranged her hair and looked out of a window."

Jezebel is one of the most misinterpreted persons in the Bible. She has always been referred to in the fact that she put on makeup and adorned herself, when she heard that Jehu was coming to Jezreel. The spirit of seduction that she carried should be noted. Generally, women who get dressed up and adorn themselves in a provocative manner for men, are consequently looked at as being a type of Jezebel or having a Jezebel spirit.

However, there is a more substantial take on the spirit of Jezebel. It is at its core, controlling and manipulative. Control and manipulation has no gender. It is of a truth that Jezebel used her role as a woman to enhance her control and manipulation, but both men and women can control and manipulate others. In other words, both men and women can operate in the spirit of Jezebel.

Definitions:

MANIPULATE: to control or influence (a person or situation) cleverly, unfairly, or unscrupulously.

CONTROL: the power to influence or direct people's behavior or the course of events.

PSYCHOLOGICAL MANIPULATION: a type of social influence that aims to change the behavior or perception of others through abusive, deceptive, or underhanded tactics.

Jezebel definitely operated using the spirit of control and manipulation. She controlled people by riding off the influence of someone else. In her case, that someone else was her husband, King Ahab. She was also the daughter of a King. So, she was used to being empowered by a higher source of authority.

Even at her death, after Jehu had her thrown out of the window and she died, he commanded that they go and properly bury her because she was a King's daughter.

2 Kings 9:34 NIV

"³⁴ Jehu went in and ate and drank. "Take care of that cursed woman," he said, "and bury her, for she was a king's daughter."

The spirit of Jezebel is usually tolerated within the church. This is allowed due to the ineffective leadership style, communication, or influence thereof, in certain areas of leaders and their leadership role (not in its totality). Allow me to bring clarity to this a little bit, because it is a hard reality.

The Bible says in the book of Revelation:

Revelation 2:20 KJV

"²⁰ Notwithstanding I have a few things against thee, because thou sufferest that woman Jezebel, which calleth herself a prophetess, to teach and to seduce my servants to commit fornication, and to eat things sacrificed unto idols."

God does NOT want the spirit of Jezebel to be tolerated. Even though God will deal with Jezebel, He (God) is not pleased with those who choose to tolerate Jezebel. The moment that the spirit of Jezebel is discerned, it is to be quickly dispelled, dismantled, excommunicated, taken down, and rebuked. If Jezebel is tolerated, the problem is no longer Jezebel, it is the person that chooses to tolerate her. God said, "I have this against you, that you tolerate the woman Jezebel." The spirit of Jezebel should never be tolerated, instead, rebuked so that the person that is being used can be restored, if possible.

The Spirit of Jezebel's true assignment is to turn the leader's heart away from God. There is not a woman in the Bible that is spoken more wickedly of, than the woman Jezebel. She is the symbol of all the wickedness of women. Jezebel is not only wicked by herself, but her wickedness affects other people and causes others to turn their hearts from God, when they already know how to be righteous.

King Ahab was King over all of Israel, but he still did not have the influence to get Naboth to give him the vineyard. Here is how Jezebel responds to him:

1 Kings 21:7 KJV

"7 And Jezebel his wife said unto him, Dost thou now govern the kingdom of Israel? Arise, and eat bread, and let thine heart be merry: I will give thee the vineyard of Naboth the Jezreelite."

She went behind his back and sent letters to the people of Israel to have Naboth killed, and she did it in King Ahab's name along with his official seal. She needed his seal of approval and influence in order to get the job done.

Jezebel, cannot be Jezebel, without being empowered by a source of power higher than her. However, most people who tolerate Jezebel do not realize that they are really empowering her and that they have the power to dispel and dismantle her.

1 Kings 21:8 KJV

"⁸ So she wrote letters in Ahab's name, and sealed them with his seal, and sent the letters unto the elders and to the nobles that were in his city, dwelling with Naboth."

Jezebel ruled the kingdom through her weak husband, Ahab. Because he married a woman that ruled him, he listened to his wife more than he listened to God. Every leader must be aware of the spirit of Jezebel; it can be a man or woman. It is a spirit that does not respect or honor authority. It is a spirit that undermines the authority of the leader. Or at times, plays along like they have the leader's best interest at heart, all while they have an alternative motive.

She wanted to rule the kingdom through the leader. In my experience, many women that do not respect their husbands embody this spirit. When a woman does not respect her husband, eventually she will not respect you as the leader. She has no honor at all when it comes to authority. Her husband is her puppet and she wants the leader to be her puppet, as well.

Jezebel is also the wife that leads the man of God, out of worship. A leader must be very aware of who they connect to in marriage. It is not to be taken lightly. When leaders choose a mate, not only should you look at the other person's qualities and characteristics, but you also have to consider your assignment. Is this person the right person, for my assignment? Jezebel was the wrong person for King Ahab. Instead of being his helpmate, she wanted to be his boss.

As a result of King Ahab marrying her, he began to serve and worship Baal. The wrong choice of spouse in leadership, will turn your heart away from God and your God-given assignment, and will change the direction of your life and your destiny, if you are not careful.

I have heard it for years, "Oh, I love the wife, but that husband..." or vice versa. The person you marry is a direct version of yourself, because the two become one. Jezebel controlled and manipulated her husband, stole property, and had people killed, all for her own personal gain. She had a direct assignment from Satan to kill off the Lord's prophets.

1 Kings 18:4 KJV

"⁴ For it was so, when Jezebel cut off the prophets of the Lord, that Obadiah took an hundred prophets, and hid them by fifty in a cave, and fed them with bread and water)."

Jezebel was wicked; she was a murderer, sexually immoral, and demonic. Her spirit was so powerful that even in Revelation 2:20, you can still see her operating and working her manipulation and control from the book of Kings, to the book of Revelation, and in the church today. Spirits can move from generation to generation. They are not limited to, or controlled by time. You can pick up a spirit at any time.

In order to succeed, Jezebel must be attached to a leader, in order to gain influence. Some people want to control God's kingdom through their leader and you have to be aware of that controlling spirit. Personally, I have dealt with this spirit when people have said to me, "Pastor, if you do not change this, I am going to leave or I am not going to pay my tithes..." however, I had to let them leave, because I know that God is for me, not against me and He would not let me fail.

Jezebel only had power because she married Ahab. You have to be careful of whom you lend your influence. Some people will only love you, because they can manipulate and control others through you. It is sad when a leader becomes a puppet and their spouse is the puppet master. A solution to handle this is praying, fasting, examining, and investigating any person that you intend on having a relationship with, in which will lead to a lifelong commitment.

Jezebel is a spirit that is unwilling to cohabit peaceably with anyone. If you are in a relationship with someone that has a problem with everyone and a fault with everything, they are under the spirit of Jezebel. Many people only think this spirit refers to sex or sexual immorality. It is beyond makeup and a short dress. This spirit will isolate you from everyone.

Before you know it, it is just you and the spirit. She will never let you fulfill your God-given call and purpose.

The spirit of Jezebel hates prophets and true leaders of God that she cannot control. She hates the word of God, praise, and worship. You can be sitting in church, next to someone with this spirit. You will notice that they will point out anything that will keep you from true worship. Their only job is to destroy the worship to the true and living God.

When you see signs of this spirit, obey the signs. Stop, recognize it, and dismiss it from your life. Do not fall in love with Jezebel. She will separate you from order, your covering, your friends and family, and lock you into a world in which you can only depend on her. This has been her trick, down through the years.

When this spirit is cornered, it will paint its face and behave as if it is innocent. In order to kill it, the spirit of Jehu must come upon the leader. Jehu looked past the flesh of Jezebel's jewelry and makeup and had her thrown out the window, and trampled over by eunuchs.

2 Kings 9:30, 32-33 KJV

"30 And when Jehu was come to Jezreel, Jezebel heard of it; and she painted her face, and tired her head, and looked out at a window. 32 And he lifted up his face to the window, and said, who is on my side? Who? And there looked out to him two or three eunuchs.

33 And he said, Throw her down. So they threw her down: and some of her blood was sprinkled on the wall, and on the horses: and he trode her under foot."

Jezebel lost, when Elijah prayed fire down from the heavens against the prophets of Baal and Jezebel's scheme and the praises of God filled the air. When dealing with the spirit of Jezebel, you have to be careful not to let your flesh get involved at all, or otherwise, she will talk you out of it.

Think about this, eunuchs were castrated before puberty; they were unable to perform sexually or have children. How powerful is the spirit of Jezebel, that Jehu had to use men that had been castrated in order to deal with her? You have to use a pure, Godly conscience. She will do more damage than more people would think she was capable of because many people underestimate her. She is a spirit that will never negotiate and never stop. If you do not deal with this spirit, the innocent casualties will be great. Leaders, get Jezebel out of your life, immediately, Selah.

The Spirit of Delilah

Delilah is best known, in the Bible as the one who brought about the ruin of Samson. She lived in the Valley of Sorek, which lay on the border between the territories of the ancient Philistines and the Israelite tribe of Dan. Samson, one of the judges of Israel, had an affair with Delilah and she betrayed him to the Philistines. In this case, her prey, Samson, was an easy target. He knew that he was called by God to be a Nazarite, which was a clean and pure calling. However, he wanted to be ordinary and be around ordinary people, while being common with everyone.

Samson hung out with Philistines (unclean people) and never valued who he was called to be. As a result, he was an easy target for the spirit of Delilah. She had one purpose in

Samson's life, which was to discover his weakness and vulnerability through manipulation and use it against him. Hired by the Lord of the Philistines, Delilah began her assignment pressuring Samson to find out where his strength lied. After many attempts before he revealed his weakness, you would think he would be wise enough not to tell her, even though she pressured him. However, when someone is a skilled manipulator, it is hard to realize what is unfolding before you.

Before the enemy blinded Samson physically, he was blinded spiritually. Samson allowed Delilah to put him in a compromising position, in which he got comfortable and was caught off guard. A leader must always protect his anointing and his weaknesses. People that follow the leader do not need to know every personal and intricate detail about a leader's life. Privacy is a powerful virtue, especially when it comes to a leader.

You must protect your personal life and your privacy and know whom you can be personal with and whom you cannot. Normally, it is not with those that follow you. Sometimes, leadership can be very lonely and you can lead a secluded lifestyle, because there are individuals that have one purpose only, which is to find out your weaknesses and exploit them.

Here is where many leaders are stuck. If there is an issue in your life, sometimes you have no place to go. Sometimes you cannot even trust Christian counselors. Jesus has to be your comfort, counselor, motivator, and instructor. You must use His word to bring you through many of life's challenges. I am not saying you cannot get counseling, but you must make sure it is a reliable, integral, and confidential consultation.

Delilah aggravated and manipulated Samson so much that he made up stories in order to pacify her. Samson first told her he that had to be tied up, in order for his strength to disappear. But, he broke through the restraints when the Philistines came to get him and in return, destroyed them. The second time she asked, Samson told her more lies and once again destroyed the Philistines. The third time, Delilah made a big deal about it and Samson eventually told her that his strength lied within his hair. As a result, he was destroyed by the Philistines.

Samson's strength came from God. He was so blinded by his love for Delilah and her cunning manipulation, that his common sense never kicked in. He did not understand that Delilah was selling him out to the Philistines. He continued to deal with her, in spite of the attacks on him after revealing his "secrets" to her.

Sometimes, a weakness of a leader includes their commitment to a person that is no longer good for them. Leaders have to use discernment. Even though the Holy Spirit gives the gift of long-suffering, sometimes a leader can delay it because of their unwillingness to remove bad spirits from their presence. Do not become a victim of the spirit of Jezebel and Delilah, you could find yourself in a world of trouble.

Chapter Seven

Herodias' Venom

Every leader, at some point, will challenge a spirit or have to correct someone regarding one thing or another. Correction is too hard for some, because they are bastards and not sons of God.

Hebrews 12:8 KJV

"8 But if ye be without chastisement, whereof all are partakers, then are ye bastards, and not sons."

King Herod the Great was a Roman King of Judea, born in Indumea. He is known for his descendants who also functioned in leadership roles as Kings. Herod Archelaus, Herod Antipas along with their father Herod the Great are referred to as the Herodian Dynasty in Christian literature. They are similar to the Divine Dynasty of Kings when the era of the Kings first began with Saul, David, and Solomon.

Allow me to mention something about leadership, in ancient Biblical times. Many times, leaders and rulers inherited their positions. This means that they did not necessarily live a lifestyle devoted to God or the commandments of God. That is why the Deuteronomist would say "And he did that which was evil, in the sight of the Lord."

2 Kings 23:37 KJV

"³⁷ And he did that which was evil in the sight of the Lord, according to all that his fathers had done."

2 Kings 24:19 KJV

"¹⁹ And he did that which was evil in the sight of the Lord, according to all that Jehoiakim had done."

Such was the case with the Herodian Dynasty. They were Romans that were converted to Judaism, but did not live fully devoted to the teachings of the Law. They pretended to be righteous around real scholars and people of the law. Not only that, but at times, Jews were a bit Pharisaic themselves.

Pharisaic is a direct correlation to the Pharisees, they practiced and promoted a strict observance of rituals and ceremonies, but they were not circumcised in their hearts. King Herod the Great ordered the slaughter of all infants during the birth of Jesus Christ.

Matthew 2:16 KJV

"16 Then Herod, when he saw that he was mocked of the wise men, was exceeding wroth, and sent forth, and slew all the children that were in Bethlehem, and in all the coasts thereof, from two years old and under, according to the time which he had diligently inquired of the wise men."

The Herodian Dynasty is quite complex, because of the time in which they lived and their conversion. Keep in mind that Jerusalem was an occupied country at this point. A Roman government, during the time of Jesus, occupies Jerusalem. King Herod's people were Romans who were converted to Judaism and their ancestors were wicked.

These Kings oppressed the people of God at the same time they claimed to have been converted to Judaism. King Herod the Great was responsible for killing his wife and two of his sons. He was also responsible for the building of Herod's Temple.

Herod Antipas was the King of Galilee, during the time of John the Baptist. Jesus referred to this king, as a fox. In the book of Luke, the Pharisees seek to warn Jesus about Herod's wrath and Jesus response to them was:

Luke 13:32 KJV

"32 And he said unto them, Go ye, and tell that fox, Behold, I cast out devils, and I do cures today and tomorrow, and the third day I shall be perfected."

Jesus referred to King Herod Atipas as a fox because of his reputation of cruel, tyrannical leadership throughout his lineage. Don't get me wrong, the Herodian Dynasty accomplished great things. Among them, was the temple they built for the Jews. However, they built other buildings for other religions, and oppressed the Jewish people. This particular bloodline had a wicked history and no one dismantled it.

King Herod Antipas had John the Baptist beheaded because of Herodias, the wife of his (King Herod's) brother. Herod married his brother's wife and John the Baptist spoke out against it. As a result, Herodias had a grudge against John the Baptist and wanted him dead. However, Herod did not want to have John the Baptist killed, because he knew John the Baptist to be a man of God. However, the King was manipulated into having to do something that ordinarily, he would not have done.

Mark 6:17-24

"**17** For Herod himself had sent forth and laid hold upon John, and bound him in prison for Herodias' sake, his brother Philip's wife: for he had married her.

18 For John had said unto Herod, It is not lawful for thee to have thy brother's wife.

¹⁹ *Therefore Herodias had a quarrel against him, and would have killed him; but she could not:*

²⁰ *For Herod feared John, knowing that he was a just man and holy and observed him; and when he heard him, he did many things, and heard him gladly.*

²¹ *And when a convenient day was come, that Herod on his birthday made a supper to his lords, high captains, and chief estates of Galilee;*

²² *And when the daughter of the said Herodias came in, and danced, and pleased Herod and them that sat with him, the king said unto the damsel, Ask of me whatsoever thou wilt, and I will give it thee.*

²³ *And he swore unto her, whatsoever thou shalt ask of me, I will give it thee, unto the half of my kingdom.*

²⁴ *And she went forth, and said unto her mother, what shall I ask? And she said, the head of John the Baptist."*

During my tenure as a spiritual leader, I have corrected people in love and in righteousness, because they did not have the proper relationship with God. The venom I got back was lies, scandal, and persecution. Because these people did not have the proper relationship with God, they were not able to receive the correction that I was giving to them. Never be afraid to pull the trigger on correction. If you lose someone because of it, they were never meant to be in your life and that is why God exposed them.

Herodias never received the correction that was given to her. Her venom was holding onto anger and she ultimately wanted John the Baptist to be destroyed for correcting her. She knew she was wrong and waited until the right time to have her daughter, Salome, order his head on a platter.

Some people are so wrong that they cannot handle correction being handed down to them. This spirit is present as it relates to a leader, no matter what field you are in. Beware leaders, by correcting someone, you could potentially have a lifelong enemy. I corrected someone twenty years ago, and to this day, they still hate me. Correction can birth lifelong enemies and leaders must be up for the challenge.

Chapter Eight

The Spirit of Saul Venom

Definition:

PRIDE: 1) A feeling or deep pleasure or satisfaction derived from one's own achievements.

2) The quality of having an excessively high opinion of oneself or one's importance.

There is no doubt that Saul started out right, in his role of leadership. One of God's best men, the Prophet Samuel, accompanied him. Saul was also sent to a company of Prophets. And the Bible said that Saul also prophesied so much that the people began to say, "Is Saul among the Prophets?"

1 Samuel 10:11 KJV

"11 And it came to pass, when all that knew him before time saw that, behold, he prophesied among the prophets, then the people said one to another, what is this that is come unto the son of Kish? Is Saul also among the prophets?"

Saul was from the tribe of Benjamin, a small tribe of Israel. God chose him by to be King of the children of Israel, because they had rejected God and desired a King. Many people like to point to Saul's jealousy of David, but Saul became haughty and prideful way before David killed Goliath. Saul had some very humble beginnings. When the Lord presented Saul to the Prophet Samuel, Saul did not hesitate to tell Samuel of how small of a tribe he was from, and how they were small in number and substance. How humble this conversation was:

1 Samuel 9:17-21 KJV

"17 And when Samuel saw Saul, the LORD said unto him, behold the man whom I spake to thee of! This same shall reign over my people.

18 Then Saul drew near to Samuel in the gate, and said, tell me, I pray thee, where the seer's house is.

19 And Samuel answered Saul, and said, I am the seer: go up before me unto the high place; for ye shall eat with me to day, and tomorrow I will let thee go, and will tell thee all that is in thine heart.

20 And as for thine asses that were lost three days ago, set not thy mind on them; for they are found. And on whom is all the desire of Israel? Is it not on thee, and on all thy father's house?

21 And Saul answered and said, Am not I a Benjamite, of the smallest of the tribes of Israel? And my family the least of all the families of the tribe of Benjamin? Wherefore then speakest thou so to me?"

The Lord gave Saul and the children of Israel victory over certain nations, long before David's season of triumph. Saul's victories got him into trouble. Saul's great achievements gave him a deep pleasure of self-satisfaction and a high opinion of himself that led him to disobey the Prophet Samuel.

God gave Saul victory over the Ammonites and then they attacked the head of the Garrison of the Philistines. When they did that, the Philistines declared war on the children of Israel but Saul did not heed the voice of

Samuel. His instructions were to wait seven days for Samuel to arrive and make sacrifices unto the Lord. Instead, Saul made the sacrifice himself and this displeased God, as well as Samuel.

What would cause Saul to do such a thing? The people of God scattered in fear of the Philistines, and Saul felt he needed to do something as King to bring consolation to the people. This particular event was an act of pride. How dare Saul not wait on the Prophet of God and obey the instructions of the Lord in its entirety. God had given him victory and was with him and on his side, but he felt the need to step outside of the plan of God and do something that he was not qualified to do, which was make sacrifices.

1 Samuel 13:11-12 KJV

"11 And Samuel said, what hast thou done? And Saul said, because I saw that the people were scattered from me, and that thou camest not within the days appointed, and that the Philistines gathered themselves together at Michmash;

¹² Therefore said I, The Philistines will come down now upon me to Gilgal, and I have not made supplication unto the LORD: I forced myself therefore, and offered a burnt offering."

Saul was given a commandment to go and smite the Amalekites and utterly destroy all that they had and spare them not, but slay both man and woman, infant and suckling, ox and sheep, camel and ass. Saul disobeyed God by allowing the people to keep the spoils, sheep and oxen, and said that it was for the people to make sacrifice unto the Lord. Saul thought that he had God all figured out and that he could get the same results as Samuel, by making sacrifices. However, God does not delight in burnt offerings and sacrifice. He is delighted in our obedience!

1 Samuel 15:21-23 KJV

"²¹ But the people took of the spoil, sheep and oxen, the chief of the things which should have been utterly destroyed, to sacrifice unto the LORD thy God in Gilgal.

22 And Samuel said, Hath the LORD as great delight in burnt offerings and sacrifices, as in obeying the voice of the LORD? Behold, to obey is better than sacrifice, and to hearken than the fat of rams.

23 For rebellion is as the sin of witchcraft, and stubbornness is as iniquity and idolatry. Because thou hast rejected the word of the LORD, he hath also rejected thee from being king."

There was a significant level of jealousy towards David that King Saul exercised. However, I want to point out the pride of Saul before David came along, because Saul had issues in his leadership role before David became a matter of contention. After David killed the Philistine Goliath, the people began to sing his praises and Saul's heart was wrought with jealousy. Remember, David was ruddy and attractive, but his fame was the ideal factor that also weakened the leadership of Saul.

1 Samuel 18:7-8 KJV

"7 And the women answered one another as they played, and said, Saul hath slain his thousands, and David his ten thousands.

8 And Saul was very wroth, and the saying displeased him; and he said, they have ascribed unto David ten thousands, and to me they have ascribed but thousands: and what can he have more but the kingdom?"

Many times, leaders can be intimidated by talented and gifted individuals that serve under them. This is a poor leadership quality and some leaders will do things to hold gifted, influential people that serve under them, down. This was Saul and David's problem. Saul knew that David had God, more God than he ever had.

The spirit of jealousy and envy took over Saul's decision-making and made him an ineffective leader, because of David's influence and capabilities. Any great leader should facilitate great people under them. The venom of jealousy and intimidation is a major attack on any leader that is intimidated by someone else's relationship with God and their capabilities.

I have encountered many people that are more gifted than I am, throughout the years. I have learned to use their gifts and abilities to make the team better, rather than smothering them and holding back their gifts and abilities. It is a good thing to be a leaders, leader.

A leader has their place, as well as those that follow. There has to be teamwork. Not everyone can be the quarterback, wide receiver, or field goal kicker. They all have to feel secure in their own capabilities. When you are chosen, you are chosen for a set purpose, set position, and set agenda.

When a leader is unsure of his call, purpose, and agenda, the venom of intimidation and jealously, known as the spirit of Saul, will cause the leader to attack the gifted individuals that serve under their tutelage. In reality, nothing you do as a leader can hinder the person under you from reaching their full potential, even if you attempt to sabotage them. I have seen it repeatedly, leaders trying to sabotage those that follow them. However, God will do whatever He has to in order to ensure the continuance of the process of whom He has laid His hands on.

The intimidated leader cannot stop whom God has called to move forward. Anytime this venom comes into the leader's heart, the leader should address it by praying and rebuking the spirit, because you cannot lead correctly, unless you lead with a clear conscience, and a pure heart.

Saul was overtaken with jealousy when he saw the fame and potential of David. Another major reason why Saul constantly attacked David is because the presence of God left Saul and he saw what he once had, in a greater way, on David. From that moment on, an evil spirit came upon him. Saul had many moments of disobedience and rebellion, yet he never repented for his sins.

The former generation must embrace the growth and development of the next generation. You may as well support it, because they are the future. Secure leaders support and embrace the future. No one leader is the end all, be all.

God is much bigger and greater than one generation. He cares about our children and our children's children. As a leader, make sure your vision is big enough to facilitate the next generation. It is a small vision that ends with you, and your generation. When you have a vision from God, embrace the level, size, and length of it. Saul had a great start in leadership, being anointed by one of God's best men. However, pride, haughtiness, disobedience, and jealousy were the downfall of this once, great leader.

Chapter Nine

The Spirit of Absalom Venom

The natural meaning of the name Absalom is "Father of Peace." Absalom did not just wake up one day and decide to overtake his father's Kingdom. Absalom was dealing with many intense emotions, in the Book of 2nd Samuel.

In the Bible, the scriptures point out that Absalom has a sister by the name of Tamar. Why didn't the scripture relate Tamar to her mother or father? It specifically notes the relationship of Tamar to her brother, which is Absalom. David's son, Amnon, raped her. There is absolutely no consolation mentioned in scripture for Tamar or Absalom and no vindication. As the scripture goes on, Absalom's behavior began to depict the behavior of someone who is seeking for vengeance or some type of reciprocity. Obviously, Absalom has some unfinished business or emotions that he is expressing, through the vehicle of venom.

Venom is demonstrated within this story in the Bible, because David was furious when he heard of Amnon raping Tamar. But, he did nothing and that fueled his other son Absalom's, venom.

2 Samuel 13:12-37 KJV

"12 And she answered him, Nay, my brother, do not force me; for no such thing ought to be done in Israel: do not thou this folly.

13 And I, whither shall I cause my shame to go? And as for thee, thou shalt be as one of the fools in Israel. Now therefore, I pray thee, speak unto the king; for he will not withhold me from thee.

14 Howbeit he would not hearken unto her voice: but, being stronger than she, forced her, and lay with her.

15 Then Amnon hated her exceedingly; so that the hatred wherewith he hated her was greater than the love wherewith he had loved her. And Amnon said unto her, Arise, be gone.

16 And she said unto him, there is no cause: this evil in sending me away is greater than the other that thou didst unto me. But he would not hearken unto her.

17 Then he called his servant that ministered unto him, and said, Put now this woman out from me, and bolt the door after her.

¹⁸ *And she had a garment of divers colors upon her: for with such robes were the king's daughters that were virgins appareled. Then his servant brought her out, and bolted the door after her.*

¹⁹ *And Tamar put ashes on her head, and rent her garment of divers colors that was on her, and laid her hand on her head, and went on crying.*

²⁰ *And Absalom her brother said unto her, Hath Amnon thy brother been with thee? But hold now thy peace, my sister: he is thy brother; regard not this thing. So Tamar remained desolate in her brother Absalom's house.*

²¹ *But when King David heard of all these things, he was very wroth.*

²² *And Absalom spake unto his brother Amnon neither good nor bad: for Absalom hated Amnon, because he had forced his sister Tamar.*

²³ *And it came to pass after two full years, that Absalom had sheepshearers in Baalhazor, which is beside Ephraim: and Absalom invited all the king's sons.*

²⁴ *And Absalom came to the king, and said, Behold now, thy servant hath sheepshearers; let the king, I beseech thee, and his servants go with thy servant.*

²⁵ *And the king said to Absalom, Nay, my son, let us not all now go, lest we be chargeable unto thee. And he pressed him: howbeit he would not go, but blessed him.*

²⁶ *Then said Absalom, if not, I pray thee, let my brother Amnon go with us. And the king said unto him, why should he go with thee?*

²⁷ *But Absalom pressed him that he let Amnon and all the king's sons go with him.*

²⁸ *Now Absalom had commanded his servants, saying, Mark ye now when Amnon's heart is merry with wine, and when I say unto you, Smite Amnon; then kill him, fear not: have not I commanded you? Be courageous, and be valiant.*

²⁹ *And the servants of Absalom did unto Amnon as Absalom had commanded. Then all the king's sons arose, and every man gat him up upon his mule, and fled.*

³⁰ And it came to pass, while they were in the way, that tidings came to David, saying, Absalom hath slain all the king's sons, and there is not one of them left.

³¹ Then the king arose, and tare his garments, and lay on the earth; and all his servants stood by with their clothes rent.

³² And Jonadab, the son of Shimeah David's brother, answered and said, Let not my lord suppose that they have slain all the young men the king's sons; for Amnon only is dead: for by the appointment of Absalom this hath been determined from the day that he forced his sister Tamar.

³³ Now therefore let not my lord the king take the thing to his heart, to think that all the king's sons are dead: for Amnon only is dead.

³⁴ But Absalom fled. And the young man that kept the watch lifted up his eyes, and looked, and, behold, there came much people by the way of the hill side behind him.

³⁵ And Jonadab said unto the king, Behold, the king's sons come: as thy servant said, so it is.

³⁶ And it came to pass, as soon as he had made an end of speaking, that, behold, the king's sons came, and lifted up their voice and wept: and the king also and all his servants wept very sore.

³⁷ But Absalom fled, and went to Talmai, the son of Ammihud, king of Geshur. And David mourned for his son every day."

Absalom's venom was a result of Amnon's actions. Amnon forced himself on Tamar, his half-sister, and hated her after her raped her. However, David did not retaliate after learning of his son's wrongdoing. This scenario demonstrates how David was caught in a fatherly position. His son raped his daughter and he did not know what steps to take afterwards. What do you do in that case? Kill your son to avenge your daughter or let it all go?

In some cases, people feel that a predator has not gotten the correction that they feel the leader should have brought upon them or that the consequences were not severe enough. Sometimes, they feel the leader did not do anything about it at all, not realizing that the role of the leader is one that is held accountable for everyone on board, like a captain on a ship.

People do not realize that there are times when a leader is puzzled, especially when there are people that are dear to him and these people have a negative encounter amongst themselves. In times like this, leaders are put in a hard place and don't necessarily know how to handle the situation.

There was one instance in 2007, in which our church was growing rapidly. We had just gone onto national TV and our sanctuary had recently been completed. I received a call that a Deacon from my church had sexually assaulted one of the young women in my ministry, while she was at their home babysitting their children. She wanted to be of help to this particular family because of their dedication to the ministry and their need for a babysitter. This Deacon served in ministry and his wife also worked as an administrator with one of the ministries within the church.

This particular Deacon and his wife had moved from New York with us. I felt a certain level of loyalty towards him and his family, for being faithful to the ministry throughout the transition. As the spiritual leader of the congregation, I was very cognizant of keeping the business of the church within the church and not allowing things to become a public embarrassment. As this crisis unfolded, I approached the couple and talked to them about the alleged situation. The Deacon admitted everything to me and other leaders within the ministry, and the young woman and her family decided not to press charges against him. In cases like this, me being the leader, I could not be involved in that part of the process, one way or another.

Because of his confession, I knew I had to correct this matter within the church. So, I sent him away to another local pastor within the city, to help him get his life together. While he was away, a major spirit of rebellion began within him and he stopped showing up for his appointments.

While he was rebelling at his potential place of restoration, his wife began to rebel in her own way. She became the author of confusion among the staff within the ministry. The embarrassment of her husband's sexual assault was too much for her to handle, and as a result, her venom was created. She lashed out at me directly, and decided to start and spread rumors about me.

Now remember, I was only 33 years old at the time and this was a hurtful situation. Instead of following the directions for his restoration, the Deacon rebelled against the process that I put into place in order to cover him. We felt as a ministry of reconciliation that had no choice other than to allow him to come back to our church, after a few months. Little did we know, in allowing him to come back to the church, we created problems for ourselves and the ministry.

This was a learning experience that I encountered with that family. Instead of being grateful that we allowed them back into our church family, they plotted against me and began to make up crazy, outrageous, and outlandish stories. This was because I was the one that took out the discipline on them. I became their personal target for retaliation.

She felt embarrassed by what her husband had done to a young lady, and as a result, wanted my wife and I to feel the hurt and embarrassment that she felt.

This evil, venomous, retaliating spirit was easily conquered by having the proper leadership in place that was mature enough to ask her and her husband to present the evidence they had against me...emails, pictures, text messages, videos, anything. However, they were unable to present it and have yet to do so.

At a certain point, you have to give things and people to God, and continue to prosper and win in life. There are some enemies that will last a lifetime, but you must keep going and let those that come against you live in their unrighteousness, while you continue to live in God's grace, mercy, and favor.

You can see in this case, that people wanted the penalty for that crime to be greater from day one. But, because of my love for this family and the history between us, I dealt with them longer than I should have. Once our lawyers permanently dismissed them from the church, the story got even worse. It continued to grow, every month and every year following.

I should have been aware of the wife's character based on what she said to me about her former church and pastor, when she first joined the ministry. She claimed that her old pastor had been sexually inappropriate with her. Looking back, I now realize that there was a pattern to her actions. You should never think that someone will come to your church with false accusations and negative statements about their last church and not seek to make you and your ministry their next victim when their true character is finally exposed.

You must realize that the enemy's job is to be the accuser of the brethren. He uses his power to get leaders to lose their influence with the people. Once a leader loses their influence with the people, they can no longer lead as effectively as they once did. The enemy wants to take away the influence of leaders through lies, manipulation, and deceitfulness.

Venom is a direct result of the malice, in someone's heart. Malice births anger and anger births retaliation. When an animal uses venom as a defense, it is rightfully used, because it is self-defense. Venom is a form of self-defense for someone that has past experiences and hurt, that has been unresolved.

If you are a true leader with a genuine heart, your love for a person will never leave your heart, but you do not have to allow them back into your world. A leader's greatest defense is God, Himself. God has to be a leaders' vindication, to keep them clear from accusations, imputations, suspicions, or the like.

Chapter Ten

The Spirit of Jehu

What is the Spirit of Jehu? Who is Jehu?

The natural meaning of the name Jehu is "Jehovah is He." The natural meaning of the name Elijah is "Jehovah is God." During the reign of Elijah, Jezebel had the opportunity to repent, to cease her idol worship to Baal and bow down to the true and living God, but she refused. After many different times of seeing God's power, when it came to her destruction, God used Jehu. Jehu was nonnegotiable when it came to the destruction of her. Jezebel painted her face and tried to distract him from her judgment, by beautifying herself, and covering her ugliness with makeup.

Sometimes, when people realize their season of manipulation and control is over, they will try to disguise their evilness with a fraudulent smile, nice comment, or deed.

They will do anything to stop their final judgment. However, Jehu looked past her painted face and ultimately destroyed the spirit of Jezebel. After he and the dogs got finished with her, all that was left was her skull, feet, and the palms of her hands. Jehu was relentless in his assignment to destroy Jezebel.

2 Kings 9:35 NKJV

"35 So they went to bury her, but they found no more of her than the skull and the feet and the palms of her hands."

Jezebel and Ahab had many chances to turn to God with Elijah, but once Jehu appeared, it was only time for judgment and she received the death that she deserved. A good leader must take on the attitude of Jehu by looking past people's abilities, beauty, talent, money and gifts, and lead them based on the truth of God's word. They must be able to make decisions based on God's word and not the outer appearance of people.

Chapter Eleven

Idolatry

(Idolizing Leadership)

As a leader, I have learned to say sorry, even when I was innocent and always when it was my fault. There is no perfect leader. Leaders are human beings that have been called for a purpose or agenda by God. A smart spiritual leader will always point people to Jesus. He will always let Christ be the center of the ministry and people's focus. You must always keep Christ as the head and the light, in the eyes of the people. A leader is too human to handle the glory that should go to God. Never allow people to make you their god or hold you to standards higher than they hold God. Again, a good leader points people to God and not themselves.

Idol worship is a major problem in churches around the world today. I have also learned when you tell God's truth, some desire to hold you in a higher place than they do God. When you identify this person, do everything in your power to lower their level of accessibility to you, because the spirit of obsession can be birthed from these feelings and ideas. That is a dangerous spirit.

Definition:

OBSESS: Preoccupy or fill the mind of (someone) continually, intrusively, and to a troubling extent.

Signs of obsession:

- People cannot praise God, see God or worship God, unless you are there. If you go on vacation, they go. If you are not in service, they cannot praise God. But when you come in, the praises get high. They can only receive, if you are preaching.

- People will want the exact same things that you have such as your clothes, house, cars, neighborhood, etc.

Some leaders are ok with this spirit, but they should not be. These individuals do what they do for man, and not for God. Although that may make a leader feel good, in the end, these are signs of obsession that a leader must help break off the individual's life. Always let God be your motive. What people do for the leader let them do it, but do it as unto God.

It should be every good leader's desire to see people in a greater place with Jesus Christ and not just a greater place with the leader. Leaders cannot save anyone. So, beware of the overly-obsessed individuals within your congregation. Work on weaning them off of you and getting them addicted to the word of God and God, Himself.

Obsessions can quickly go from the greatest love to the biggest hate (Tamar and Amnon). The Bible states that he loved her, and once he raped her, he hated her. Obsession can turn the love that an individual once had, into a greater hate.

2 Samuel 13:15 NKJV

"15 Then Amnon hated her exceedingly, so that the hatred with which he hated her was greater than the love with which he had loved her. And Amnon said to her, "Arise, be gone!""

In one instance, we had an individual within our organization that was operating in major unrighteousness. One day, we received word that they were making unwanted aggressive advances on some of the brethren within the congregation. Upon confrontation, he completely denied the allegations, however, one of the brethren had recorded him trying to hit on him. So, we played the tape for him and it contradicted his denial. As a result, he was dismissed from his position.

When a person is exposed and found out, here again we see, sometimes their next move is to tell lies and attempt to scandalize your name in order to cover themselves. Regardless of their attempts to slander you, know that the stories that they tell will not prosper, instead, be confident in the fact that God will cover you, vindicate you, and you will have victory! Keep on moving forward with the vision!

Obsessive people do not want to see their leaders around anyone else, but themselves. They get upset when you are with other people in the group and, as a result, they will become needy or their mood changes if you acknowledge someone else and not them.

Sometimes as a leader, it is necessary for you to test the spirits of those around you by not acknowledging them, just to see how they react. This test is done to make sure that their hope is in Jesus and not you. Test their spirit and see what their motives really are. You can test the musicians, by telling them that you cannot pay them and see how they react. You can also test your assistants, by not allowing them to travel with you and see how they react. You can test your adjutants by not allowing them to serve with you, but instead, send them out to serve others and see how it goes. If you are faithful to the ministry, it is not just about the leaders, but also the entire team.

Leaders must also be careful with people that mimic every little detail of their life. Beware of people that want the exact same things that their leaders have. The leader must steer these people into the right direction, once these signs are revealed. In the process of leadership, I have learned that the person that has an obsession will duplicate leader's lives piece by piece and inch by inch. When they are not able to compete with the lifestyle that the leader lives, it will turn into animosity and hatred towards the leader.

They will wonder, "how do you still live there and how do you still have that, when I lost mine?" They do not realize that you have what you have, because of the favor of God on your life. They must embrace the favor that is on their life and their place of favor. Just because you follow a leader, does not mean that the favor that is on the life of the leader is the same favor that will be on your life.

Watch out for people that always have to duplicate you to extreme levels such as suits, shoes, haircuts, makeup, etc. Nine times out of ten, they are not serving Jesus, but they are potentially serving you. It is okay to serve your leader, in Jesus name. But when it becomes all about a person, it becomes a problem.

The only path if one continues in leadership obsession, is for God to set it up so that person either gets "bumped in the head," or finally finds God, so their mind can become reverberated.

Romans 1:21-23 NIV

"21 For although they knew God, they neither glorified him as God nor gave thanks to him,

but their thinking became futile and their foolish hearts were darkened. **²²** *Although they claimed to be wise, they became fools* **²³** *and exchanged the glory of the immortal God for images made to look like a mortal human being and birds and animals and reptiles."*

Do not get me wrong, you can have some of the same things. However, when every part of their life mimics yours, every move they make, the neighborhood they live in, and they wear the EXACT same suit, that is a sign that this person could possibly obsessed with you.

The earlier you address the spirit of obsession, the easier you can wean someone off you and point them in the right direction. The longer you let it go on, the harder it is to undo overly obsessive people. People should love their leader, they should be committed, and have levels of dedication, but you must determine if they love you more than they love God. If so, that is a problem that will eventually come back and slap you in the face.

Some say as long as you do what I say, or are not disrespecting me, that everything is okay.

However, they disrespect other people that you put in charge. That is not the way to think. You can tell how they think and act based upon the way they treat the lowest person; the parking lot attendant, the video team, the stage handlers, all the people in the back, and the least of them. Sometimes, this is a good barometer of a person's true heart. The greatest person that can service a leader is the person that has a true heart for God, first.

When the people worshipped God, they did not glorify Him on the level they should have (*Romans 1:21-23 NIV*). They were not thankful and did not appreciate anything, so they took the glory of God and turned it into images. Leaders have to be careful that they are not turned into an image. God is higher than any image. Do not let people make you a God. It must be addressed.

Some leaders may embrace it for a season, but once it all goes downhill, the people will not blame God, they will blame you. For twenty years, I have taught people not to put confidence in me, but instead, keep it in Jesus. God is the only one that will not fail you. Man may fail you, but God will not. Keep your eyes on Jesus.

Chapter Twelve

The Spirit of Lucifer

Revelation 12:10 NKJV

*"10 Then I heard a loud voice saying in heaven,
Now salvation, and strength, and the kingdom
of our God, and the power of His Christ have
come, for the accuser of our brethren, who
accused them before our God day and night,
has been cast down."*

Lucifer was a chief angel in heaven. One day,
he attempted to exalt his throne above the
throne of God. As a result, there was a war in
heaven. He and the angels that followed him
were kicked out of heaven. Sometimes, there
isn't a place left for people that cause a lot of
trouble within a place. Just like Lucifer,
sometimes people can do something in
ministry that is so devastating that there is no
longer a place for them.

Revelation 12:7-9 NKJV

*"7 And war broke out in heaven: Michael and his
angels fought with the dragon; and the dragon
and his angels fought, 8 but they did not prevail,
nor was a place found for them[a] in heaven any*

longer. ⁹ So the great dragon was cast out, that serpent of old, called the Devil and Satan, who deceives the whole world; he was cast to the earth, and his angels were cast out with him."

People with the spirit of Lucifer are not interested in you, but rather in your position and they want to be back in their position. This is a strong area of attack, because of the spirit of Lucifer. This spirit will identify someone that is on the way to promotion and it is aware of the gift, within that individual. As a result, they befriend the individual, take interest in them, and do things to make them think that they are a good friend, in order to deceive them, but, it is not genuine. At face value, it looks good, but their actual motives aren't. Their intent, is to ensure you never fill that spot or are removed from that one that you are in.

When Satan leaves, he wants an entourage to follow. It is not enough to go by himself. He wants to go out with a bang!

Lucifer deceived one third of the angels in heaven, and were banished with him. People that carry this spirit will leave your organization and still be obsessed with connecting with people that are still there, with the intent of utilizing deceptive tactics in order to eventually have them removed from their position with the intent of having them abandon their ordained assignment.

Any place other than where God told you to be, is in the wrong place. That spirit can see where you are going and they will notice the favor on your life. You may feel like you are barely making it, but they see God's favor on you from afar. They want the influence and power that you, the new person, possess from God.

In addition, leaders should not be surprised when known enemies become friends just to come against you. They build a team, in order to take you down. You give them something in common to come against, so they will find ways to attempt to dethrone you. If they are unable to succeed, they will still get together just to defame and slander you.

It is a strategy of the spirit of Lucifer to divide and conquer and it happens all the time. Lucifer was truly a gifted musician. How much more can he influence humans that are not angels, against God and God's plan? Blaming the leader because of your faults is not the right way to do it. To rise up against what God has set up, is not the way to handle things.

If God has put a person in place, that is their position. Lucifer's wickedness runs deep. His deception is powerful. He was able to take a THIRD of the angels in heaven, with him. So, you must be aware of this spirit. We have to be governed by the word of God and not our feelings. Feelings can feel right in the moment, but what does the word of God say about that issue.

There is always a right and wrong way to do things. People that operate under the spirit of deception will delight in scattering congregations. These are things that God does not like. As a matter of fact, sowing discord is something that God hates. So, if your time is up and you are leaving your place of worship, make sure you leave correctly. Leave in a manner that maintains your dignity and integrity.

On the other hand, as a leader, you have to know when it is time to dismiss someone from the team or your church. Because of Lucifer's dismissal from heaven, he has a job to deceive the nations of the world to kill, steal, and destroy all of us who now benefit from the God that he attempted to overthrow.

So, BEWARE of people that lost their position and have been dismissed from your organization. The spirit of Lucifer will cause them to be envious of their replacement, just because they have taken their place. They will try to get them out of their position from working under their leader, because they are upset that someone new has the position that they once had. To intimidate them, they will try to discourage them, in their new position. Lucifer wants his seat back, but because of his offense, he cannot return.

Chapter Thirteen

Overcoming False Accusations

Now more than ever, in the 21st century, people can say anything, anywhere, at any moment, and build an audience. In these days and times, everyone tends to believe everything that they read on the worldwide web. The internet is the murder capital of the world. Your audience is broader and bigger.

You can get online and get an audience of thousands within minutes, based on your conversation. The internet is something that my father, grandfather, and great-grandfather never had to deal with. Therefore, it is very important, when you are dealing with, following, and supporting leadership, to handle crisis and accusations, biblically.

The Bible helps us, with resolving and dealing with these issues. It says:

1 Timothy 5:19 NIV

"19 Do not entertain an accusation against an elder, unless it is brought by two or three witnesses."

God has already put in place a system to find truth in matters, accusations, lies, conflicts, and scandals and it is based on the accounts of witnesses. Any leader that operates in truth and righteousness is always susceptible to false accusations (the enemy's job is to kill and destroy the truth). The best defense to any lie is the truth. Knowing the truth will set people free. That is Satan's number one job, to create accusations against the brethren.

Here is a simple solution: if people that follow leaders hear an accusation about their leader would take the time to ask the accuser to prove their accusations, you would be waiting for years upon years, in many cases, for that proof to surface. The criminal justice system wants physical, circumstantial, or testimonial evidence, in order to prove a suspect of a crime. So, why shouldn't you?

The Bible teaches us that two to three witnesses must establish every word. It is up to us to follow its teachings. Stop believing in junk, without having any proof. If someone has an accusation against a leader, they must be able to prove it. Many accusations could end, if we were responsible enough to follow the scriptures and do not believe something, because we hear it or read about it on the internet.

Quick story: In the past, there was a member of my church that had many bad things to say about the leadership within our congregation. So, one of our senior elders approached them and heard their concerns. As a result, the elder asked the person for proof of their claim and for them to back up their accusations.

Once the person went to retrieve the information, they never came back. The ministry never heard from that person again, because they were unable to back up the stories that they were telling about their colleagues. If we would only request proof during these situations, we would find out that many of these stories that people insist on telling, are not actually true.

Notice, if you call a meeting and the accusation is false, the liar will never show up. The proof is in the pudding. In my experience, liars don't usually show up to meetings, if they do appear, they are quickly proven as the false accuser.

Revelation 12:10

"10 Then I heard a loud voice saying in heaven, Now salvation, and strength, and the kingdom of our God, and the power of His Christ have come, for the accuser of our brethren, who accused them before our God day and night, has been cast down. 11 And they overcame him by the blood of the Lamb and by the word of their testimony, and they did not love their lives to the death."

John 8:44

"44 You are of your father the devil, and the desires of your father you want to do. He was a murderer from the beginning, and does not stand in the truth, because there is no truth in him. When he speaks a lie, he speaks from his own resources, for he is a liar and the father of it."

It is also important to be aware of your brother and sister's attacks. It is the enemy's job to divide us and keep us against each other. If he succeeds, the will of the Father will not be done in ministry. Accusations will slow down progress. You can't build, grow, develop, or become the powerful force on earth that God has called you to be in ministry, if we embrace these types of spirits designed to slow down leaders, and stop productivity in the church. What you give life to will live. What you ignore will starve and die.

I can recall a time, in 2006, when Pastor Richard Hogue from TBN called me on stage, during a live taping of my wife's first on-air interview. He advised me that there was a bull's-eye on my back. From that moment, my warfare increased. My attacks got greater. Previously, I only had local attacks, but from that moment forward, they became global. High levels of exposure can cause high levels of attack.

We live in a world that no longer values truth. This world has turned truth into lies and people would rather believe in lies. However, we live in a world where people get off, by putting people on "blast." The warfare of today is different, because everything is done in public.

In my twenty years of experience, I have rarely ever publicly addressed lies and scandals. I have used the pulpit to pull people out of the pit and for the message of Jesus Christ, but not to deal with defending myself. Every time someone gets inspired by Satan to slander my name, I constantly stay focused, so Satan gets no airtime.

If he does not get airtime, he moves on. That is how I overcome many things, by not giving it life or airtime. When I have had conflicts that I felt needed to be addressed, I only did it amongst my leadership team. This way, they were aware of what was occurring. Then, they were able to relay the truth to any individuals that may have mentioned it to them.

You also have to be careful about what you release publicly these days. Sometimes, you have to go public, but not always. It depends on the severity of the incident and its importance.

You have to measure if what someone says really affects you, and if people are feeding into it. Most people that know you will know what to believe and what not to believe. They may have the rumor, but God has the record.

Above all, you must stay with the assignment. Nehemiah kept building, in spite of his attacks. Keep building and stay focused. Do not be distracted or deterred by taking your eyes off your assignment. I never make a lie a big deal. I allow liars to die with their lie, while I live with the truth.

Chapter Fourteen

Knowing Whether You Are in a Church or a Cult

In the sociological classifications of religious movements, a cult is a social group with socially deviant or novel beliefs and practices.

Cults Often:

1. Control their members every move.

2. Get a new revelation from God, or claim God has shown them a new doctrine.

3. Keep their members prisoners, by use of threats.

4. Tells anyone that disagrees with them they are headed to destruction and damnation.

5. Isolates members from family, loved ones, friends, etc.

6. Make members dependent on the cult or cult leader for everything.

Do not allow people on the outside of your church, to confuse good leadership or good spiritual covering, with a cult. Understand there are some bad leaders, just like there are bad doctors, lawyers, dentists, real estate agents, police officers, and teachers. But there are also good doctors, lawyers, dentists, real estate agents, police officers, and teachers.

Hebrews 13:17 NIV

"17 Have confidence in your leaders and submit to their authority, because they keep watch over you as those who must give an account. Do this so that their work will be a joy, not a burden, for that would be of no benefit to you."

In the pastoral ministry for instance, a pastor must teach you the truth, be an example of the truth, celebrate you when you are doing good, and correct you when you are doing wrong. It is their responsibility to give an account to God for your spiritual life, growth, and progress in the word of God.

Your responsibility is to submit to the spiritual authority, receive their spiritual teachings of the scriptures and look at their example of life. This is the responsibility of pastoral leaders, to the people that they serve.

It is not their job to tell you what to eat, who to marry, what to wear, or where to work, among other things. That is too much involvement. Pastors feed the people the word of God, live the example of godly leadership, celebrate those that delight in righteousness, and correct those that do unrighteousness. After this, their job is done. Pastors cannot make anyone do right. Individuals do right by the conviction of the Holy Spirit, and pastors cannot do the job of the Holy Spirit.

The truth of cult leaders cannot be found in the scriptures. The pastoral truth and leadership methods however, can be found in the Bible. The best way for someone to know if they are in a cult or under good leadership, is to reference the Bible and compare them to the teachings of your leader.

Cult leaders create brand new doctrines and revelations that are inspired by man instead of God. They claim that this new doctrine or revelation is from God, but this cannot be proven. For example, beware of male leaders with a First Gentleman instead of a First Lady. BEWARE of new revelations that are not supported by the Bible. They do all of this in the name of forward thinking, a new wave of the future, or may be known as a progressive movement. Any new doctrine that removes the truth of the word of God from their teachings, is a cult!

Chapter Fifteen

RESET

Definition:

RESET: 1) To move (something) back to an original place or position.

2) To put back into the correct position for healing.

In the twenty years that I have been a pastor in three major cities, over four churches, I have learned that is it not wise to do some things myself personally in ministry, but to instead, stand behind the board of my church.

Correcting or even firing people individually makes everything seem personal, instead of as an institution. Sometimes, leaders should delegate the authority of correction instead of doing it themselves, in order to protect your leadership. This was learned when I corrected people in the past personally, and I am still a recipient of their venom, today. But, that is okay.

Now I am responsible for five churches, in five major cities. As an Overseer, I have learned that it is necessary to reset and move forward with your life, after the hurt. I learned how important it is to never stay in a place of defense or hurt. Leaders must be quick to forgive and let go and not hold on to past offenses. I once heard someone say, "A leader must be quick to forgive, and let a situation go." Holding on to unforgiveness is like drinking poison and waiting for the other person to die.

In leadership, in order for leaders to live and operate in purity with a clear conscience, a leader cannot hold onto the offense of someone that has mistreated them. In order for people to get the full benefit of your leadership, they must see the example of forgiveness and restoration inside of the leader.

Restoration is the hardest part, because people say they forgive you all the time. However, can you really forgive and restore that person, every time? Leaders must be able to restore those that have gone astray and fully bring people back to their positions because God is the God of full recovery.

This is why God told Jeremiah to root up, tear down, destroy, and build again. In order to do that, the leader must be sensitive to God, sensitive to people that follow them, and sensitive to individual's personal life transitions.

Leaders that are easily offended are usually poor leaders, because people that carry offense never take the time to reason. They automatically question things and feel that others are being malicious. Leaders have to handle individuals based on that individual and no one else, not that last person that did that same offense to them.

When I was younger, I used to say that certain people acted like others. I soon realized that it was not the person, but a spiritual thing. These spirits have travelled to different places and jumped into different people. These spirits will attach itself to anyone that will allow it. As leaders, we have to focus on the spiritual side. Certain spirits will attach itself to our assignments, no matter where we are located. Spirits are not subject to particular territories. There is a spirit that is an enemy to every leader's assignment.

It is an assigned spirit to destroy that leader's progress, growth, and influence. You are only a leader, because of your influence. If the enemy can steal your influence, then he has you.

Leaders must also do everything that they can in order to avoid burnout. Whenever you are short fused, snappy, edgy, have short responses, or are sleep deprived because of your never-ending to-do list, get away by yourself or with your spouse. Take a vacation to refresh, renew, and spend time with God and yourself. This can be a couple of days or a month. Know your limits.

Reset by praying for God's wisdom, direction, cleansing, and power, so you are not contaminated by any of the experiences around you. This includes spirits, negative attitudes, and more. Sometimes, people will tell you everything that is going on in their life and unload all of their problems onto you. As a result, you are contaminated by people's problems, issues, and baggage. Just because you are a leader, it does not mean that you are exempt. Take time for yourself and let God reset you.

Chapter Sixteen

The Leadership Test

Author Jon Mertz believes that people would like their leaders to be both tested and inspiring. He feels that this leadership combination creates the right mix, in selecting the prudent paths forward, weathering the challenges ahead, and lifting up a higher purpose. He believes it causes orientation, in the work to be done.

A tested leader is someone who has experienced victories and defeats and most other places in between. More than experiencing these situations, is successfully and unsuccessfully working through them. In success, there are insights, just as there are in unsuccessful experiences. The key for a tested leader is that they have grown in what they have learned from both.

An inspiring leader is someone who lifts the spirits of another and rallies people to do more than they thought possible. Inspiration raises one's view to see what is possible and what the larger purpose means. An inspiring leader knows how to tap into the human spirit and use it to achieve a higher goal and mission.

As a leader, you are often tested by spirits, people that serve under you, and those that are above you. The key to being an effective and long-lasting leader is being able to lead in a variety of situations and with a variety of different people.

The first thing that is often tested is a leader's authority. There will be those that try to question your authority. Always be secure in who God has ordained you to be. God supports your authority. Promotion doesn't come from man. God chooses an individual to be a leader.

Psalms 75:6-7 NIV

*"⁶ No one from the east or the west
or from the desert can exalt themselves.
⁷ It is God who judges:
He brings one down, he exalts another."*

Even if people are not in agreement with your authority, God is the head of your life, not man. People can only reign as king or ruler, by the authority of God.

Colossians 16:1 NKJV

"**16** For by Him all things were created that are in heaven and that are on earth, visible and invisible, whether thrones or dominions or principalities or powers. All things were created through Him and for Him. **17** And He is before all things, and in Him all things consist."

You have been created, for a purpose. If you are sitting in a seat, holding a position of authority, your authority comes from God. God makes men rulers and says who is in charge to bring about the purpose in His will in the earth. Never question the position that God has placed you in. A confident leader is a good leader and you have nothing to prove to anyone.

It is better to be a God pleaser than a people pleaser. God set you up to win and not fail. Always seek Him as your refuge, your counselor, your defense, your everything. No matter what position you are in, your authority first comes from God.

The second thing that is tested is faithfulness. A leader must be found faithful to the assignment and the mission, even without anyone else's participation. Good leaders are examples of faithfulness. They are faithful in supporting the vision, faithful in investing in the vision and faithful in endurance in the vision. Leaders have to show up, when no one else does. They must speak positively, when everyone else is negative. Remain focused when everyone else is unfocused and never lose hope or motivation in the vision.

Hebrews 10:36 NIV

"36 You need to persevere so that when you have done the will of God, you will receive what he has promised."

Proverbs 28:20 NIV

"20 A faithful person will be richly blessed..."

Matthew 25:21 NIV

"21His master replied, 'Well done, good and faithful servant! You have been faithful with a few things; I will put you in charge of many

things. Come and share your master's happiness!"

The third thing that is tested is integrity. Our integrity was really tested, in one instance back in 1997. We had recently started our church and the bills were really starting to pile up. There was the mortgage, utilities, insurance, maintenance fees, taxes, and other bills that we now had on our plates that we had not, previously.

One day, we invited a guest pastor to come and preach for us. After the service, as we were making small talk, he told us that he and his congregation did not pay those types of bills and he had a person that could "hook us up" with free gas and power. He went on to explain that we could use the "additional" money we had "saved" for the ministry in other areas that needed attention. Initially, I told him to contact me a few days later, so that we could start the process. However, by the time that day came around, God had warned me that we were not going in the same direction as them, and we had to do things with integrity in order to prosper.

As a result, we turned down his help and decided to continue to carry on in the direction we were going, no matter how tight things got. In this, I learned that not all help is from God, even though, it may be for a Godly purpose. You must maintain your integrity, in spite of the need that you may be facing.

About two years later, that church closed down and that pastor is no longer leading. God was right, we were not going in the same direction and because of his grace and mercy, we are still going strong twenty years later. Never align yourself with other leaders that do not uphold the same standards as you. You have to have integrity, with God and with man.

Philippians 4:19 NIV

"*19 And my God will meet all your needs according to the riches of his glory in Christ Jesus.*"

Psalms 84:11 NIV

"11 For the Lord God is a sun and shield;
the Lord bestows favor and honor;
no good thing does he withhold
from those whose walk is blameless."

The fourth thing that is tested is your obedience to God and not man. This was another one of the initial challenges that I encountered. God told me to instruct the church to do something and some of the people in my congregation did not agree with it. Thankfully, I was able to stand secure in the instruction that God gave to me and remained firm in my decision. As a result, many people left my church, but we managed to survive the exodus of several key members of the ministry.

When you are obedient to God and His word, you will always land on your feet. The ministry will not only survive, but thrive. Leadership will survive insurrection.

Deuteronomy 28:1-2 NIV

"¹If you fully obey the Lord your God and carefully follow all His commands I give you today, the Lord your God will set you high above all the nations on earth. ² All these blessings will come on you and accompany you if you obey the Lord your God:"

Chapter Seventeen

Covering and Praying For Your Leader

Definition:

KASAH (כָּסָה): To cover.

Genesis 9:23 KJV

"⁹And Shem and Japheth took a garment, and laid it upon both their shoulders, and went backward, and covered the nakedness of their father; and their faces were backward, and they saw not their father's nakedness."

The word covered, in this particular text, is **Kasah (כָּסָה)** in Hebrew. It means to cover, to conceal, or to hide. At this point of the book, I would like to take the time to address the responsibility of sons and daughters to cover their leaders. Whenever you think of leadership, it is almost automatic that one would think that a leader has the responsibility to cover and to protect the people that they lead. However, it is very seldom mentioned, the responsibility of sons and daughters in the ministry or subordinates of any kind of leadership, to cover their leaders. Addressing this topic is crucial to the Body of Christ at large, as well as to corporate America.

In the church, we hear this phrase a lot "Who is your covering?" In essence, who are you submitted to in ministry, who is leading you and giving you spiritual guidance en route to your destiny? Who is shepherding you? Ultimately, that answer is the name of a LEADER, PASTOR, or someone of spiritual authority. That person is responsible for your welfare and making sure you have the proper spiritual nutritional diet.

While I understand and agree with that, I am also aware of the lack of COVERING from sons and daughters and lay members to take on the responsibility to actively COVER their LEADERS (pastors, supervisors, or group leaders). In this day and time, I see people more or less place their leaders on a pedestal and watch them fall from the very high expectations that they have set for them.

Let's take a look at Noah's sons and see from their example what we could gather from them. Noah had three sons, Japheth, Shem and Ham. Noah who is their father is obviously their leader and not only that, but he is God's Man. God is pleased with Noah and decides to use Noah to spare a remnant on the earth, while He destroys it because of sin and disobedience. Noah's entire family gets spared because of his faithfulness to God. When God gets done, Noah becomes a planter and begins to replenish the earth by planting. Noah's drinking caused him to be intoxicated.

Genesis 9:20-21 KJV

"And Noah began to be a husbandman, and he planted a vineyard: And he drank of the wine, and was drunken; and he was uncovered within his tent."

Noah has obviously indulged a little too much and was found unclothed. The scripture uses the term uncovered. This does NOT take away from his leadership at all, neither does it erase all that God has done through Noah. All it shows is the humanistic existence of any leader, their frailty, and dependence on God, of whom is our source. The responsibility of his sons NOW, is to have their father, their leader's back, and cover him, in this situation. The reaction of Noah's youngest son Ham was NOT the proper response. He saw his father uncovered and had no regard for him, but to go and tell the other two brothers who made sure that they did NOT SEE their father in that state. They loved their father enough to COVER him up, so that NO ONE ELSE could see his nakedness!

Proverbs 10:12 KJV

"Hatred stirreth up strifes: but love covereth all sins."

The Apostle Paul often admonished the church to continue to acknowledge, consider, and give thanks to God, for their leadership. Because it is through the mouthpiece of leadership that God deposits and releases breakthroughs for the people of God. Paul constantly reminds the church to NOT make the job of leaders grievous.

Hebrews 13:7 AMP

"Remember your leaders [for it was they] who brought you the word of God; and consider the result of their conduct [the outcome of their godly lives], and imitate their faith [their conviction that God exists and is the Creator and Ruler of all things, the Provider of eternal salvation through Christ, and imitate their reliance on God with absolute trust and confidence in His power, wisdom, and goodness]."

There is a stigma that comes with honoring leadership. Unfortunately, people like to abase, degrade, and diminish the idea of reverencing leadership. They speak against titles and positions and obedience to leadership. There is a variety of reasons for this mentality. I will name two dominant reasons.

1. Pride - people are too prideful to honor and respect and serve one another, especially people of authority.

2. Perversion - many positions of leadership have functioned without integrity and have perverted their

authority as leaders, by being drunk with authority.

As a result of these two things, the idea of honoring leadership has been distorted in the minds of many. The enemy has strategically used these two demonic and anti-authoritarianism tactics that oppose leadership and seeks for its own liberty, apart from Christ. However, covering leadership is a responsibility that we all share. We cover them through love, obedience, and care.

Hebrews 13:17 AMP

"17Obey your [spiritual] leaders and submit to them [recognizing their authority over you], for they are keeping watch over your souls and continually guarding your spiritual welfare as those who will give an account [of their stewardship of you]. Let them do this with joy and not with grief and groans, for this would be of no benefit to you."

Not only does God want us to submit to them by recognizing their authority as God given authority, but understanding how they are held responsible and are held accountable for us by God. There is an anointing and a grace on the leader to perform the works of God.

The leader is wired differently than his subordinates and laymen. When the children of Israel fought against Amelek in the book of Exodus, it was Moses their leader who held up the rod before God. As long as Moses held the staff up to God, the children of Israel prevailed. But when he lowered the staff, Amelek prevailed. The hand of God was upon Moses and he was a mediator, between God and the children of Israel.

In this particular passage of scripture, three people played a very important role in winning the battle between Amelek and the children of Israel. It was Aaron, Hur, and Joshua. These three people were watchful and positioned themselves in the right place, to get the job done. Joshua was obedient to choose people to go out and get their hands dirty to fight. Aaron and Hur followed Moses to the hilltop and were attentive enough to Moses to recognize when he grew fatigued. They were ready to assist by propping him up and holding his arms.

The Leaders' 7 Deadly Venoms

Do you see the team work? LEADERSHIP TAKES A TEAM.

A team of obedient people who do not mind getting their hands dirty and checking for one another and are attentive to THE LEADER, the set man in charge, the man that God has his hands on, is ideal. This is necessary for a leader to be covered correctly.

Exodus 17:8-13 AMP"

"8 Then Amalek [and his people] came and fought with Israel at Rephidim. 9 So Moses said to Joshua, "Choose men for us and go out, fight against Amalek [and his people]. Tomorrow I will stand on the top of the hill with the staff of God in my hand." 10 So Joshua did as Moses said, and fought with Amalek; and Moses, Aaron, and Hur went up to the hilltop. 11 Now when Moses held up his hand, Israel prevailed, and when he lowered his hand [due to fatigue], Amalek prevailed. 12 But Moses' hands were heavy and he grew tired. So they took a stone and put it under him, and he sat on it. Then Aaron and Hur held up his hands, one on one side and one on the other side; so it was that

173

his hands were steady until the sun set. [13] So Joshua overwhelmed and defeated Amalek and his people with the edge of the sword."

There is an anointing to cover leadership. When you obey and cover leadership, God will give you the ability to defeat the enemy just like He did Joshua. Joshua defeated Amelek because he was obedient to leadership. Covering leadership through OBEDIENCE was exactly what Joshua did. Covering leadership by being watchful and attentive towards him, was the action of Aaron and Hur. Earlier, when I discussed Noah and his sons (Shem & Japheth) they covered leadership through their integrity.

Genesis 9:23 KJV

"[23]And Shem and Japheth took a garment, and laid it upon both their shoulders, and went backward, and covered the nakedness of their father; and their faces were backward, and they saw not their father's nakedness."

Be someone that covers your leaders just as they cover you. While you may know that they have targets on their backs, you may not have known the extent of their attacks until you read this book. Be someone they can count on to uplift, uphold, and raise the standards of those around you. Choose to cover your leaders when they may be exposed. Choose to be a Shem and Japheth – not a Ham. Choose to lift them up when they grow weary. Choose to be an Aaron, a Hur, or a Joshua in this season... choose to be great!

About the Author

Bishop Orrin K. Pullings, Sr. is the founder and Chief Prelate of the United Nations International Church Fellowship. Under his leadership, United Nations Church International has expanded to encompass churches in Jamaica, NY; Richmond, VA; Atlanta, GA; Charlotte, NC; Fredericksburg, VA and a host of fellowship churches in North America. A man of great faith, Dr. Pullings is the author of the biblical and inspiring book *"Unstoppable Faith."*

As a noted community leader and humanitarian with over 20 years in leadership, Bishop Pullings is a sought-after international conference speaker, pastor, teacher, televangelist, and life-coach, changing the lives of people; motivating them to believe in God for the impossible both naturally and spiritually.

Bishop Orrin K. Pullings, Sr. is the proud husband of Dr. Medina Pullings and father of their five children - Orrin Jr., Elijah, James, Zacchaeus and Medina.